DEATH BY SARCASM

MARY COOPER MYSTERY #1

DAN AMES

FOREWORD

Do you want more killer crime fiction, along with the chance to win free books? Then sign up for the DAN AMES READER GROUP:

AuthorDanAmes.com

DEATH BY SARCASM

by

Dan Ames

Sarcasm is the last refuge of modest and chaste-souled people when the privacy of their soul is coarsely and intrusively invaded.

-Fyodor Dostoyevsky

Sarcasm is the language of the devil.

-Thomas Carlyle

There's a fine line between fishing and standing on the shore looking like an idiot.

-Steven Wright

1

Instead of the local rats, a team of crime scene technicians scurried around the grimy alley, popping flashbulbs and taking notes. Occasionally, blue and red lights flashed on the cinderblock walls, courtesy of the black-and-whites blocking each end of the alley.

Mary Cooper stood next to her uncle's body. The large pool of blood – to her it looked like a Snow Angel from Hell - had already thickened, turning darker as if its purity had been contaminated by the lingering sins of the alley's sordid past. And even though the club was just a few blocks from the Pacific, the air held a thick pall of L.A.'s favorite aromatherapy scents: rotting garbage, human piss, and death.

Mary had said nothing upon her arrival. Now, several minutes later, the uniforms were starting to sneak glances at her, wondering how long she planned to maintain her silent vigil. They unconsciously positioned themselves closer to her, just in case her grief and rage exploded and they needed to restrain her in order to protect the sanctity of the crime scene.

In the alley behind some two-bit comedy bar called the Leg Pull, Brent Cooper had been shot in the head. A large, deep cut had been made across his belly. The knife, a long, bone-handled stiletto was then thrust into the body; its perfect verticality looked like an exclamation point to Mary. And the knife held in place a note.

The words on the paper were in thick block letters, probably from a Magic Marker.

Bust a gut.

Mary tore her eyes away from her uncle and glanced up at the officer now standing directly in front of her, watching her. His eyes seemed to implore her to express her emotions, but in a calm, measured way. She could guess what he was thinking. That maybe she would tell him a cute little story about how her uncle used to swing her in the air and threaten to withhold ice cream if she screamed. Or maybe she would tell him how her uncle used to insist on reading 'Twas The Night Before Christmas every year in front of a crackling fireplace near the twinkling tree. But Mary offered no tidbits. For one thing, Mary had no such stories. Nobody would ever confuse their family with the Cleavers. And while there was definitely grief, and an abundance of rage, she had used the time observing her dead uncle to unclench her fists. To slow her racing heartbeat, and to gather her thoughts. She pushed aside her own feelings and coolly observed the crime scene. Took in the facts of the murder. But at some point, she knew she had to say something to the uniforms.

So then, at last, she turned to them and spoke.

"Are you sure he's not just asleep?"

2

Detective Jacob Cornell emerged from a dark section of the alley and nodded to the uniform guarding the crime scene. Cornell was a big man, with a considerable physique, and a handsome-ish face. Not the kind that would land him on the cover of GQ, but certainly could find him a place in a Walmart flyer modeling $7.99 flannel shirts. Now, he wore a sportcoat that camouflaged his powerful upper body, and khakis that hid the ankle gun Mary knew he always wore.

"Jesus Christ, Mary, he's your uncle...was your uncle," he said, his voice a whisper. "I mean, I called you here because I thought you would want to know. I mean, I know it's not my place, but, a little respect, a little decorum..." His voice trailed off.

Mary nodded in agreement, as if she was glad she'd been properly admonished.

"True, true," she said. "That's a very, very good point, Jake." She paused. "It's just that he was always such a heavy sleeper. It runs in the family." She cut her eyes over at him, winked, and said, "You know that."

Jacob Cornell closed his eyes and held them shut for a beat. And then when he opened them, he looked at her with a sideways glance. "This is not the time and it certainly isn't the place," he said, his voice soft.

Mary felt warmed by his indignity. A little pissed that he was judging her, but she was used to that by now. Nobody would ever liken her to an open book. But still, despite his many faults, an overly developed sensitivity chief among them, Mary didn't mind knowing someone like Jake. So good. So nice. So friggin' cute.

"I'm not sure why you're focusing on me, instead of my dead uncle lying over there in repose," Mary said. "But since you're questioning me, I ought to remind you that he was a comedian, Jake," she said. "Believe me, if the roles were reversed, he'd be standing right here saying, 'What's the big deal? I've died hundreds of times at comedy clubs – but it was always *on stage*.'" She pantomimed a rim shot. "Boom ch," she said.

One of the crime scene technicians looked up from his notepad at Mary. She caught his gaze and held it until he looked back down. Jake pulled out a notepad and tried to hide the guilty look on his face.

"Come on," she said to him. They walked to the end of the alley and Mary looked west, toward the ocean. She couldn't see anything. Just a vast darkness. She turned and caught her reflection in the store window. Did she look like a woman who'd just identified the corpse of a family member? She studied herself, saw a lean woman with a strong face wearing an expression that was open to interpretation. Just the way Mary liked it.

Jake broke into her thoughts. "A waitress on her smoke break found him," he said, still speaking softly. "She ran back in and…"

"Was he already dead?"

Jake hesitated, then said, "She thinks he may have been...twitching a little."

Mary nodded. Her hands involuntarily formed themselves into fists. She forced them back open, willed them to relax.

"So she runs in, calls 911, then finds the manager and they go out together," Jake continued. "By then, he's definitely dead."

"Had they seen him inside? Before?"

"We're talking to everyone now," he said. "A few people thought they saw him at the bar, having a drink. A couple others thought he might have done a couple minutes on stage. But no one knows if he left with someone or by himself."

"Who was on stage when he was there? Who was performing?"

Jake looked at her, his face blank. "Umm...I'll have someone check on that."

"Might be worth looking into," Mary said. "Maybe he came specifically for the show. He'd been around comedy clubs for a long time. Maybe he knew the headliner–"

"Oh, shit," Jake said, his breath going out of him with a rush. The pen froze above his notepad. He looked directly behind Mary, over her shoulder.

"I'm sorry to hear about your loss," a voice said. Mary felt the chill of recognition and her stomach turned sour. She turned and came face to face with Jacob Cornell's superior. Mary should have known the woman would show up.

"Sergeant Davies," Mary said, her voice calmer and more in control than she would have thought possible. "I almost didn't recognize you with your clothes on."

Arianna Davies was tall, thin, and pale. Her black hair

was cut short. Mary knew that her nickname around the squad room was The Shark. Davies had a well-earned reputation as an apex predator. Now, Mary's comment hadn't even caused her to dilate a pupil. Mary noticed, however, that Detective Cornell looked like he wished he could liquefy himself and slide down the storm drain. It was the exact same expression he'd had on when Mary let herself into his apartment only to find The Shark literally eating him alive.

"Ah, I see that at least the Cooper wit still lives on," Davies said.

Mary felt a spark of anger flash inside her, but she held her face still.

"And speaking of unwanted interruptions," the Shark said to Jake. "I assume you were interviewing Ms. Cooper." The way Davies raised her voice at the end made the statement both a question and an indictment.

"Actually, we were just finishing up–" Jake said.

"Good." Davies turned to Mary and spoke in a flat monotone. "You have our deepest sympathies. We will keep you up to date with the progress of the investigation. You will not do any investigating of your own. If you are observed anywhere near this case, you will be arrested and your private investigator's license revoked. Is that understood?"

Mary seemed to absorb Davies' speech with thoughtful concentration. Then she turned to Jake and gestured with her thumb back toward Davies.

"I thought these new robots were equipped with better voice modulators," she said.

Mary wound up at a dive bar on Ocean Boulevard that had been there since the Rat Pack was big.

Three strong drinks later, Mary looked at herself again in the bar mirror, remembering the young cop standing across from her, her dead uncle between them. The cop had looked at her, expecting her to choke out through great sobs a heart-touching story about the old man. Goddamnit, she didn't have any stories. Uncle Brent had been a first-class smart-ass, just like everyone else in the family. He'd made her laugh a couple times, though. Like the time he'd told their church lady neighbor that he'd been up in Hollywood, making porn movies. Uncle Brent claimed to be making five movies a day, ten bucks a shot. He'd said his stage name was Dickie Ramms.

Mary had been in high school around that time, and she had nearly pissed her pants. Now, she suddenly started at her reflection. Mary was shocked to see a smile on her face, and even more stunned to see moisture around her eyes. It was leaking out onto her cheek. She brushed it away with the back of her hand.

"Quiver," she said, replaying the family tradition when someone was about to cry. "Come on, quiver," she said to her reflection.

And that Davies? Come on. What in the world was Jake thinking? She was all wrong for him. Christ, if he wanted a sheet of plywood he should have just gone to Home Depot. Maybe he had some kind of weird fetish for women resembling corpses. Necrophilia Lite. Uh, God, she thought. She felt nauseated over the thought of a corpse. Her uncle. Fuck. What a shitty way to go. The anger came back, and she welcomed it. It was much better than the self-pity she was on the verge of diving into.

The bartender walked over and noticed her expression.

"Everything okay?" he asked. Mary thought she saw a touch of actual caring, along with a healthy dose of good old-fashioned curiosity.

Mary wiped her nose. "No, everything's not okay. I just lost my uncle."

The bartender started to offer his condolences, but Mary cut him off.

"But," she said. "I haven't looked under the fridge yet."

The bartender paused, then walked away, shaking his head. Mary shrugged her shoulders. There were people who got her. And there were people who didn't.

She'd long since given up trying to figure out who was who.

4

Hey Brent, what are those photographers shooting? Your last head shot? Damn. Felt good to see that bastard julienned in the alley. It'd felt even better to stick the knife in him, to see the shock on his face.

I'm sitting a block away at a little Coffee Beanery, watching the death parade. The rats actually found him first. Maybe even gnawed a little on the body before someone called the cops.

Revenge was a dish served best over and over again. Third, fourth, fifth helpings. Keep it coming, baby.

Cops don't have a clue, either.

You're the first bookend, Brent.

Start off big, with one of the leaders. Sandwich a few of the sheep in between, then end big with the other bookend.

The set-up and then the big punch line.

Who's laughing now, asshole?

Who's laughing now?

Mary parked her Buick in front of Aunt Alice's house. The Buick was just one of her cars. She had a Lexus when she needed to meet with clients or set up surveillance in the wealthier part of L.A. She also had a Honda Accord when she needed to blend in as an employee of a firm downtown. They were parked in the garage back at her office. When she needed something really expensive, say a Porsche or a Ferrari, she just rented it. But Mary used the old Buick for occasions that took her into the financially depressed sections of L.A.

The great thing about the Buick was that even though it was old, it didn't have many miles and it had surprisingly smooth power. Still, she'd endured quite a bit of heckling for it. A woman just north of thirty driving a Buick. She'd heard it all. Was the trunk big enough for a full case of adult diapers? Had she gotten an AARP discount? What was the dual temperature control for – menopausal hot flashes?

The sad thing was, most of those jokes had been her own.

Now, the morning sun warmed her back as she stepped

onto the porch of the small house in a quiet part of Santa Monica. Alice Cooper had lived there for forty years. She and her husband bought the house back when she was acting and doing comedy. Alice's husband had died of cancer, an agonizing two-year battle. Alice had kept both the house and her maiden name.

While Alice's career had never recovered, the southern California real estate market certainly had. Right now, Alice probably had the lowest property taxes in town. When, and if, Alice ever sold the place, she'd be a very wealthy woman.

Mary gave a quick knock, unlocked the door with her key, and walked inside.

Aunt Alice sat in the living room with the television off and a scrapbook in her lap. She was in a wheelchair, one arm in a cloth sling, and one leg in a brace. The older woman had been riding her motorized three wheeler when she'd hit a parked car and flipped over it, onto the hood. Mary had always been a frequent visitor to the house, but ever since the accident, she'd been stopping by every day.

"Hey there Evel Knievel," Mary said. "Want me to line up some barrels outside? Go for the record?"

Alice shook her head. "Always a comment. Even now." But a small smile peeked out from the corner of her mouth.

Mary gave her aunt a hug and took in the comforting scent she'd known since she was a kid: laundry detergent and a hint of garlic. Mary glanced at the scrapbook in Alice's lap and she saw an old picture of Uncle Brent. Mary rubbed Alice's back and her voice softened. "How are you holding up?" she said.

Alice sighed, shook her head, and flipped the page of the scrapbook. "One day at a time, I guess."

"Want some lunch?" Mary said.

Alice said nothing, just studied a picture in the scrapbook even more closely.

"How about I whip up a rump roast?" Mary said, heading to the kitchen. "Or a butt steak. Butt steak sound good?"

"When did you first realize you enjoyed abusing the elderly?" Alice said.

"I don't actually enjoy it," Mary called from the kitchen. "It's really more of a calling."

Alice wheeled herself closer to the kitchen so neither one had to shout.

Mary took the box of Mac 'n Cheese from the cupboard and ripped it open. "So I thought I'd start by searing some foie gras," she said, then set a pot of water on the stove to boil. She set the dried pasta and packet of cheese on the counter. Mary detested Mac 'n Cheese, had had it maybe twice in her whole life when she was a kid and went to a friend's house – it was never served in her own.

Mary had tried in vain to convince Aunt Alice to let her make real macaroni and cheese, the old fashioned way with good cheese and really good pasta, but Aunt Alice insisted on the boxed crap for lunch. Old people just get into routines, Mary told herself when she finally gave up. They fall into routines, then they fall down stairs. It's all a part of nature's aging process. All part of God's master plan.

"Don't forget my vitamin," Alice said.

Mary tipped a shot of Crown Royal into a small glass, added an ice cube and a splash of water, then brought it to Alice. Her aunt lifted the glass. "To Brent."

Mary clinked an imaginary glass. "To Uncle Brent."

"Butchered in an alley," Alice said. "I keep waiting for the punch line."

"He was probably waiting for one, too," Mary said. "I

imagine he was spouting off, making a joke out of it, Cooper style."

The two remained in silence for a moment, both of them imagining Brent's last moment.

"You can't kill me yet!" Alice said, lowering her voice to do the impression of her brother. "I just plugged the meter!"

Alice drank down the last of her whiskey before speaking. "It just doesn't make any sense to me. He could be a dick, we all know that. But why would anyone want to kill him?"

You have no idea how true that really is, Mary thought to herself. *Bust a gut. Real funny.*

"Let the police figure that out," Mary said. "You focus on those parked cars."

Alice shook her head. "I think Brent was getting funnier as he got older. I think the dementia improved his sense of humor."

"Dementia?"

"Did I say dementia? Maybe I meant demented. I don't know."

Mary realized her aunt was having a senior moment while accusing another elderly person of having senior moments.

"His sense of timing needed help, too," Alice said. "Remember that time at Gladys Fitwiler's wedding? That horrible joke in front of the wedding party about the donkey show?"

"Ah, yes. A classic Cooper moment. Bestiality jokes involving the bride always go over so well at weddings," Mary said.

"Mortifying," Alice said. "And how the hell would he have known? He'd never been to Mexico."

Mary went into the kitchen, drained the pasta and

added the cheese packet, then put the noodles on a plate and brought it into the dining room. She wheeled Alice into her spot and got them both glasses of iced tea.

For the first time, Alice spoke quietly. "Now I know that car was moving."

"What car?" Mary asked.

"The car I ran into. Or should I say, ran into me?"

Alice started eating her pasta, but Mary stared at the older woman.

"What do you mean it ran into you?" she said. "You never told me that."

"Well the young officer made me feel like such a fool I didn't think I should bring it up again. Dementia might be getting to me, too. You know, the other day I thought my neighbor's shrub looked like Henry Kissinger…"

"Aunt Alice," Mary said, her voice firm, but sharp. "Please tell me what happened."

The old woman's face wore a look of tired futility. "It's like I told the young officer. I was riding my bike and saw the car. I was going to pull around it. I looked over my left shoulder to check my blind spot and then bam! I hit that darned thing. But there was no way *I* could have run into *it*, I'd looked over my shoulder when I was still a good fifteen feet away. That car backed up into *me*. And fast."

Mary stared at her aunt.

"What?" the old woman said.

Mary didn't answer, her mind sifting through the possibilities.

"I have to go," Mary said, and started to clear her plate. "Set the alarm after I've gone, okay?"

"Wait," Alice said. "You're still going to give me a bath, right?"

Mary sighed. "All right. I was hoping you wouldn't

remember," Mary said. "Would you like the exfoliating botanicals today? Or perhaps the lavender pumice?"

"Can I have both?"

Mary looked at her evenly.

"Do I need to remind you how I feel about the elderly?"

Photographs don't lie. They deliver the truth. The truth in all of its naked glory, Mary thought, studying the spread of snapshots showing a beautiful woman riding a handsome man like he was a Brahma bull at the county rodeo.

"Well," her client said. He was an entertainment attorney, a very prominent one. He was tall, with thinning brown hair and gold-rimmed glasses.

Mary had been referred to him by one of her other clients. The entertainment industry was very compact. She had broken into the circle of lucrative clientele on a quiet case of kidnapping, divorce style. Mary had brought her client's child back safe and sound, all without the press even getting a whiff.

Now, she watched as her current client studied the pornographic images of his wife and best friend, waiting for him to absorb the photograph's contents. Mary had been a private investigator for well over ten years. Initially, she had thought about becoming a police officer, but after her criminology degree she took a job working for a local investigative service. She found the work interesting and despite the sometimes tedious stakeouts, rarely boring. And since her time in the field, she'd seen it all. Including plenty of clients faced with a cheating spouse. They all reacted differently. It took some folks longer, some of the brave ones faced it right away. She sensed this guy wouldn't waste time.

Her client gave a bitter smile. "She said she was taking night classes," he said.

Mary nodded. "Well, she's certainly studying anatomy right here," she said, tapping one of the photos.

Her client went pale, and Mary silently cursed herself. It had just slipped out, but that was the problem. They were always slipping out. Besides, she had just been reminded of some infidelity in her own life. Jake and his boss. Mary had taken that about as well as this guy was taking it.

"You were highly recommended," the man said. "Your discretion, loyalty, and tenacity were called second to none." His face was pale and an edge crept into his voice. "Your bedside manner, however, was not listed as one of your strong suits. I see why."

A couple comments popped into her head, mostly about bedside manner, but this time she didn't let them slip out.

"I'm sorry," she said. She couldn't tell if he really believed she meant it, but she did. She just didn't know how to tell him. Like her bedside manner, 'opening up' wasn't one of her strong suits. "This probably won't help, but you know it's rarely about the spouse," Mary said. "Usually they're looking for something that's lacking inside themselves." Mary thought about what she'd just said. What was Jake lacking? Besides a backbone.

"It's okay," her client said, looking again at the photographs. "How disgusting. Clive and I play basketball together."

Clive clearly preferred going one-on-one with Beverly, but Mary didn't offer that up for discussion. It was a rare moment of self-editing.

"I know it isn't easy," she said. It always went this way. Cuckolded spouses, both male and female, always focused on the friend or the neighbor or the co-worker. Rarely ever the cheating spouse. Probably to distract them from the depth of the true betrayal.

Her client stood, took out his checkbook, and scribbled out a check. He ripped it off with a controlled fury and dropped it onto her desk.

"Thank you," he said. "I trust you'll save those if litigation becomes necessary."

"Absolutely," Mary said. Sometimes they wanted a copy of the pictures to brood over while getting shitfaced. Some couldn't wait to get away from them.

Mary cleared her throat. "If you know of anyone looking for a private investigator, please feel free to recommend me." She hated doing the sales pitch, but it was a necessity of the trade.

"Of course," he said, and walked out the door.

Mary wondered. That had sounded a little sarcastic.

M ary locked the photographs in her safe, then drove directly to the Leg Pull. There was still just enough daylight for Mary to get a good look at the place. In the sunlight, the club looked like a hung-over version of itself: pale, tired, and vaguely ill.

She didn't bother to go back to the alley for another look, nothing back there but bad endings. There was a part of her that wanted to wait, to get a little more perspective on the death of her uncle before she dove into the investigation. But that wasn't good investigative work. In any murder case time was of the essence. So despite the fact that the anger and hurt were still raw inside of her, she forged ahead. There would be plenty of time for contemplation later.

A bored waitress told her where she could find the club's owner/manager. She walked back to the office, her shoes occasionally making sticking sounds on the wood floor.

The door to the office was open and Mary saw a slim bald man with a pencil thin moustache. He had on silk pants, a wrinkled silk shirt, and cologne that could double as a pesticide, which probably made a lot of sense in this dump.

There was a cheap desk sign, probably handmade, letting visitors know the manager's name was Cecil Fogerty. He reminded Mary of Al Pacino's brother in The Godfather.

"What's up Fredo?" she said.

He looked at her blankly.

"I'm Mary Cooper," she said. "I want to talk to you about the murder last night."

He looked her up and down, without shame.

"Cooper? Did you say your name's Cooper?"

"You can hear."

"What are you, Brent's daughter?"

"I'm actually his pimp," Mary said. "I want to find out who destroyed my property. They owe me at least three tricks' worth."

He gave a weird little laugh that sounded like rodents scurrying behind a wall.

"Nah, you're related to Brent, I can tell," he said. His little eyes shone with the pride of his intellect.

"Actually, I'm his niece."

"Niece, huh? He never talked about you."

Mary looked around Cecil's office. Tiny, cramped, and the walls filled with photos of celebrities you just couldn't quite place. Mary tried not to notice the smell of Cecil's horrible cologne combined with stale cigars and body odor. And she tried not to think about this place being the last stop, the end of the line for Uncle Brent.

"Yeah, well I didn't really talk about him a whole lot, either," she said. "At least, until he got slaughtered behind your club."

Cecil didn't know what to say so Mary filled the void. "Why don't you tell me what you know."

"So you're not a cop, right?" Cecil said, stroking his moustache. The little eyes were shining again.

"No, but I have been known to use excessive force. But it doesn't matter what I am. I'm just a grieving niece with an attitude and not a lot of patience."

Cecil sat at attention. "Jesus, you are Brent's niece, aren't you? You don't have to get nasty, though," he said, waving his hands in an attempt at placating her. "Look, I booked him for some of the early slots, you know, sort of as a favor."

Mary took a deep breath. How far had Brent fallen that he needed favors from a crap stain like Cecil Fogerty?

"Why would you do that?" she said.

"I owed him."

Mary raised her eyebrows, indicating he should continue.

"Well, you know," Cecil stammered. "Brent was pretty good with the ladies."

Mary had known that. Uncle Brent was caustic. He used his sarcasm to hurt people. Mary had never bought into that. She believed in the power of humor to unite, not divide. But despite all that, she knew that her Uncle Brent had been quite the ladies' man. If there was something she could feel good about, it was that he probably had one helluva good time before he checked out for good.

"Frankly, I'm shocked you might have needed some help with women," Mary said. "I figured you'd tested more mattresses than Serta."

Cecil looked at her and Mary could tell he wasn't sure if it was a legitimate compliment or a whole hearted rip.

"Well..." he said, unsure if a modest agreement or honest denial was in order.

"So he helped you score," she said, urging him on and desperately trying not to picture him naked.

"You're pretty blunt, aren't you?"

"I'm as delicate as a Ming vase," she said. "So get to the part about Uncle Brent helping you with a booty call."

If sheepishness could be personified, Cecil Fogerty was now it. "Anyway," he said. "I let Brent and his buddy come in, do their thing, and I'd slip Brent like, a hundred bucks, maybe two hundred depending on the size of the crowd and how his stuff went over."

Mary let out a low whistle. "Two hundred bucks, huh?" she said, knowing it was probably only half that. "How do you keep this place running handing out that kind of dough?"

"Between Brent and the bar, it was a wash," Cecil said. "But like I said..."

"You owed him," Mary finished.

Cecil shrugged his shoulders in compliance.

"So you said 'Brent and his buddy.' What's the buddy's name?"

"No clue – never met him. I hired Brent."

For once, Cecil took his eyes off Mary's body. That's how she knew he was lying.

"Ah, the truth has such a nice ring to it," Mary said.

Cecil gave her a blank stare.

It pissed her off. Her uncle was dead. Had been cut open a stone's throw away and guys like Cecil Fogerty were still walking around.

"So you don't even know his name. You let a comic onstage, without even knowing anything about him at all? Never saw him do some material?"

"Jesus Christ," he said. "I hire the guys, I don't follow them home after they do their sets," Cecil feigned exasperation. He looked at Mary, let his eyes run up and down her body. "Maybe I could come up with something...you know...

if you want to have a drink with me." He smiled at her. Mary shuddered.

"Well, that's really tempting, Cecil, really tempting," she said. She felt the bile rise in her throat, but she forced it back down. "I bet you could put that little 'stache of yours to good use, couldn't you?"

Cecil grinned like he'd hit the MegaBall jackpot.

"We have a few drinks, I show you around the upstairs, where I've got this cool suite..." he started to say.

Mary paused for just a moment. She could let him buy her a drink, finesse a few more stories about Brent out of him. Maybe even let him take her up to his suite if she felt he had more information. She thought about that for just a moment and then pulled her stainless steel Para Ordnance .45 from her shoulder holster. She took out a handkerchief from her front pocket and wiped down the body of the gun, casually, as if she were cleaning her eyeglasses.

"I hate dust," she said. "I really ought to do more than just a surface cleaning, though. I really ought to fire a few rounds, then give it a good cleaning."

She looked up at Cecil. "You got anything around here I could shoot?"

"This isn't necessary..." he started to say.

"Let me ask you something, Cecil," Mary said. "Do you think if I shot you in the head, and then looked inside your skull through the bullet hole that I would see the name of this comedian? The name you're keeping from me?"

Mary could practically see the little moustache fibers on Cecil's face twitching in fear.

Cecil backed away from her. "Okay, okay! Talk to Jimmy! Jimmy knows that kind of stuff," he said, his voice high and whiny. "I swear to God I don't know any names or locations or anything. I just pay the guys. Jimmy will be on tomorrow at four. I promise. Tomorrow at four he'll be here. He'll be able to tell you."

Mary slid the .45 into her shoulder holster.

"You sure know how to get a man excited," Cecil said, massaging his moustache.

Mary let her eyes run up and down his body, just like he'd done to her.

"Hotties like you just bring it out in me," she said.

M ary stepped outside and breathed deeply, even though it was L.A. She made a mental note to buy a nasal inhaler for use after visiting places like Cecil's office. Rinse the smell out of the nostrils.

She tried to mentally cleanse herself of Cecil Fogerty. At this point, she wanted to go back to her apartment and maybe take a long shower. Watch a movie. Forget about places like this for a little while.

But when she got to the Buick, she stopped, her breath momentarily caught in her throat. Her hand on its own volition traveled to the butt of her .45.

And then she counted the bullet holes in the Buick's windshield. There were six.

She turned and did a 360-degree turn. There was no one anywhere near the car. She reflexively checked rooftops or open windows for the barrel of a rifle. But she saw nothing.

Mary felt the anger rise again. She gritted her teeth. And then she walked closer to the car and read the note tucked underneath a piece of the windshield.

Stop – or the next joke is on you.

As she gathered her thoughts, Mary saw a patrol car pull a U-turn three blocks down.

She took out her cell phone and called Jake.

"Someone shot up my car," she said.

"Who'd you piss off now?"

"Hey, your buddies in blue are here," she said as the patrol car pulled up next to the Buick. "You might want to pull up your pants and let them know this probably relates to a certain ongoing murder investigation."

She hung up before Jake could answer and volunteered herself to the patrol officers. Once she finished answering their questions, she did her best to see if anyone had witnessed the shooting. Eventually, someone pointed out a young guy with greasy hair and thick glasses. She walked over to him.

"I've never seen a car assassinated before," Mary said.

"I saw you talking to the cops," he said. "Is it yours?"

"A Buick? What, do I look like I'm 90 years old?" she said. "I'm just curious. Like you."

They walked as close to the car as they could get,

without getting in the way of the cops. He took a closer look at the windshield. "Probably just some kids," he said. "Vandals, don't you think?"

Mary considered it for a moment. "Yeah, vandals," she said. "Old ones."

"Old ones?"

"Old people think Buicks are for them," she said. "So they hate seeing a young hardbody like me driving one. This happens to me quite a lot, actually."

The guy adjusted his glasses and looked at Mary, his eyes slightly wide with fear.

"Why do you still drive it then?" he said.

"I'm not gonna let those old bastards win, man."

He seemed to think about it for a moment, then said, "You know, now that you mention old people, I may have seen a little something. It was probably nothing, but now it makes a little more sense, maybe."

Mary felt her heart beat a little faster. She needed a break.

"What'd you see?" she said, keeping her voice bored and disinterested.

"Well, I thought I heard something weird, little pops and breaking glass. I live up on the fourth floor," he said, pointing to a building about a half a block away.

"So then what did you do?"

"Well, I walked over and saw the car, then I saw a guy a few blocks down, walking kind of fast, but trying not to look like he was walking fast, know what I mean?"

"What'd he look like?"

"I never got a good look at him." He tapped his glasses. "It was just that he had a windbreaker on. And it was a weird color. It was kind of hard to tell, but it sort of looked like a turquoise blue. But like I said, I can't see very well. And I am partially color blind."

"What's your name?" she asked him.

"Tim."

Mary nodded.

"All right, take off Tim, unless you want the cops to take you downtown and question you for half the night."

Tim virtually trembled at the thought. He turned to go, but then had a second thought.

"You know, you were bullshitting me with that old people thing, weren't you?" He squinted at her through his thick glasses.

Mary shook her head, then held up two fingers in the peace sign and hooked them into sharp claws.

"As we used to say in the Girl Scouts: Honor bright – Snake bite!"

J ake and Mary watched the Buick's front end slide up onto the LAPD tow truck. Even though the crime scene unit had done some preliminary work, the vehicle would need to be taken back to the lab to dig out the bullets and perform more intricate examinations. Because it was possibly tied to an ongoing murder investigation, Jake had arranged for a forensic full-court press.

"So you're going to need a ride, huh?" Jake said, a little smile tugging at the corner of his mouth.

"Sure will," Mary said. "Want to wait with me for the cab?"

He took that one in stride, she saw.

"Now, Mary, there's no need for a cab," he said. "The good citizens of Los Angeles would be happy to know their tax dollars were being used to give a lady in distress much needed transportation."

"It's the Jake Cornell sex tax," she said. "I don't recall seeing that itemized on my annual tax statement."

"It's listed under city services."

"Ah," Mary said. She knew Jake was kidding around, but the idea of taking her home being seen as a charitable service pissed her off just a tad. "Well, I would accept a ride," she said. "But I'm just afraid that if the Shark found out, you would have to tuck tail again like you did last night."

He rolled his eyes. "It's called being professional," he said. "You should try it sometime."

"Career advice from a guy sleeping with his boss," Mary said. "That makes sense." She pulled out her cell phone. "I'm calling a cab. You meet a better class of people that way."

"Look," Jake said. "If you let me take you home, I'll let you know a few things we've found out, okay?"

"Now you're talking." Mary climbed into his unmarked car.

Jake fired it up and they headed east toward Santa Monica and Mary's condo.

"Spill it, Shark Wrangler," she said.

"Bullet was a 9mm," he answered. "The knife was traced to a wholesaler in Gary, Indiana, but their products are often moved from retail location to retail location so it's virtually impossible to track."

Jake swung onto Lincoln and Mary caught a glimpse of the ocean when they turned onto Ocean Park.

"Any other good news?" she said.

"We're continuing to interview the waitress and trying to track down other customers who were there, but so far nothing. We have a few names we're running down, but no one's jumping out at us."

Mary nodded.

"What about you?" he said.

"The guy who shot my car may have been wearing a

turquoise blue windbreaker, but my wit is partially color blind," Mary said. "So who knows?"

Jake pulled to a stop at a red light. They were a block from the ocean and Mary could see the moon peeking out from behind the Santa Monica mountains.

"Sounds like we've both got nothing," Jake said.

"Is that what you're going to tell Davies? Maybe during a little pillow talk?"

Jake sighed. "A. We're not sleeping together so there is no pillow talk. And B. Christ, no, I won't tell her anything you say. You think I'd tell her the truth? That I gave some information regarding an ongoing investigation to a private investigator? Do I look suicidal?"

Mary smiled inside as the light turned green and Jake gunned the car. He had shared information with her that Davies would not be happy about. That was good. She liked that. She thought of saying something nice to him.

Instead, she said, "Maybe it slipped out during a particularly fierce orgasm."

Jake took both hands off the wheel to raise them in frustration. "You need to give me a break. That was a one-night stand – we were both drunk. It didn't mean anything. And it still doesn't. Besides, you and I had already broken up."

"It was an unofficial breakup. You had Davies seal the deal – with her cooker."

"Oh my God," Jake said. Mary enjoyed the fact that she could exasperate him so.

They pulled up outside Mary's condo and Jake rammed the shifter into Park. He turned in the seat to face her. "Don't act all innocent," he said. "I heard you were going around with some weird little weightlifter guy. What'd you guys do on your first date, spot each other on the squat rack?"

"The guy at my gym?" Mary laughed. "He was my trainer."

"Yeah, sure. Uh-huh," Jake said. "Probably your sex trainer." Mary loved it when he tried to get sarcastic. It was like a kid trying on clothes that were too big for him.

"The only squat thrust I've seen recently," Mary said. "Is the one Davies was doing over your goddamn wanker."

"All right!" Jake let out a fierce sigh. He put both hands back on the steering wheel and squeezed as if it were a stress reliever. "Let's just...stop talking about it."

They sat for moment before Mary spoke. She really would have liked to invite him up to her place, but didn't want to ask. It was like she'd gone too far down a one-way alley and didn't have enough room to turn around.

"And for your information," she said. "I didn't go out with that little weightlifter guy. I was worried he would chalk his hands when things got heated up. Maybe strap on that big leather belt of his."

Jake laughed softly. Mary loved to see him smile. He had a great smile, his eyes brightened and ten years fled from his face.

"You know what I don't get?" he said, glancing in his rearview mirror.

"Nose hair," Mary said. "But you're getting plenty in your ears."

"When we were together," he said, ignoring her. "You never really acted like you cared too much, you know? I mean, I figured you did, but maybe I was wrong. And if so, then I don't see why you would now."

"Who says I care now?"

"You don't?"

"I care about the truth," she said.

"Oh, the truth," he said.

"Look," Mary said. "You moved on. You made love to a woman with the personality of a cod. And we hadn't broken up yet. But if you want to maintain your innocence. Go ahead. Fine with me. Your conscience is clear, even if your ear canals aren't."

Mary swung her door open and stepped out. She shut the door then leaned in through the window.

"But even if I still cared, I wouldn't tell you."

"Why not?"

"Because you wouldn't be able to withstand the full force of my emotions – it would render you a slave. You would beg me to allow you to caress my nether regions, to gently buff my ivory butt cheeks––"

"Okay, okay, I get it," Jake said as Mary backed toward the door of her building. "Have a good night, Mary."

He pulled the car from the curb and zoomed back toward the city.

She watched him go. Well, what she had said was mostly the truth. Except for the part about her ivory butt cheeks.

They were really more like porcelain.

T he Voor Haven Funeral Home was a modest building two blocks west of Santa Monica Boulevard. Mary stood in the stuffy, overly perfumed parlor next to Alice and her uncle, Kurt Cooper, Brent's brother.

Looking at Uncle Kurt, Mary was reminded again what a cruel puppet master genetics can be. Uncle Brent had been a dashing ladies man. Uncle Kurt looked like Burl Ives after a three-month crack binge.

Kurt's son, Mary's cousin, was a twenty-three-year-old hipster named Jason. He had thick greasy brown hair and an impressive monobrow. Best of all, even with the nauseating stench of potpourri, Mary could detect the scent of marijuana that enveloped him.

In the casket next to them Brent lay in peace, with his hands across his chest and a microphone in one hand. The microphone had been Kurt's idea.

"It'll give him something to do with his hands," he'd said.

One of Brent's buddies from his condo complex stepped

up to pay his respects. He held out his hand to Kurt, who stood at the head of the line.

"He was a good man," the old man said.

"Nice try," Kurt said. "I already called dibs on his stereo." Kurt then beamed and clapped a hand on the man's back. The man was caught off guard, looking at each of them in turn, and then back to Kurt.

"Um," he said.

Mary shook her head and looked down at her shoes. They needed a good buffing. Nice leather. She had a feeling she'd be looking at them quite a bit today.

Out of the corner of her eye, Mary watched as Alice stepped forward and took the man's hand. "Pardon my brother," she said, nodding toward Kurt. "He thinks he's in a comedy sketch." She twirled her finger around her ear. "Dementia," she whispered.

Mary accepted the man's condolences as an older woman spoke to Kurt.

"He'll be missed," she said. "It was horrible, horrible what happened to him. I can't believe he's dead."

Kurt took her hand, a look of sincere grief on his face. "Well, I hope he's dead because we're going to bury him in forty-five minutes." Kurt paused, then burst out laughing.

The woman's face held a look of barely concealed horror. Alice once again tried to explain, while Mary wished she could smoke some of her cousin's weed.

It was going to be a long, long morning.

12

S t. Hugo's Catholic Church was sparsely occupied for Brent's funeral. Because of his ornery personality, Mary was surprised anyone had shown up at all. Then again, from where she was standing behind the altar in the doorway leading to the priest's quarters, she studied the visitors and saw that most of them were old. There may have been a bus from the old people's condo where Brent lived, and it was likely that some of its occupants thought they'd signed up for a trip to the farmer's market.

Mary turned and watched as Alice and Kurt argued about his behavior at the funeral home.

"What the hell are you talking about?" Kurt said. "I was in the zone, on a roll, baby! They were eating it up!" His face was flushed and he looked like he had just come off the field after scoring the game-winning touchdown.

"You made that whole thing about as dignified as one of those hookers down on Crenshaw," Alice shot back.

"Hey," he said. "Don't talk about the priest's girlfriends like that."

Mary heard a subtle cough come from behind the

priest's half-open door. Uncle Kurt was definitely going to Hell. No doubt about it.

"Listen, butthead, this is a church. Not a comedy club," Alice said. "They don't have a liquor license here. There aren't any drunks to appreciate your gags."

"They have wine, dude," Jason said. He looked at each of them for a response, when he got none, he simply shrugged his shoulders.

"Is it Night Train?" Mary said. "I'm thirsty."

"Okay, listen goody two shoes," Uncle Kurt said to Alice. "First of all, there is dignity in good humor."

"Yeah, *good* humor. I'm surprised you didn't ask one of the old ladies to pull your finger," Alice said.

Cousin Jason snickered and Mary got an even stronger whiff of dope. He must have toked up on the way over from the funeral home.

"Second of all," Kurt continued. "Some of those hookers are really quite dignified – they put a handkerchief on your lap when they blow you."

The cough behind the priest's door was a little louder this time.

"Okay, Uncle Kurt, if you're finished preparing your sermon," Mary said, and tapped her watch, but Kurt kept going.

"Listen," Kurt said. He put his arms around Alice's and Mary's shoulders, and pulled them together like a coach gathering his players in the huddle. "We've got a good crowd out there. They're expecting a Cooper style performance, so let's not disappoint them."

"It's not a show, you jackass," Alice said.

Jason wandered over and picked up a long, brass candle snuffer and turned it upside down. Mary could hear his thoughts; 'hmm, if I put the weed in here...'

"You think Brent would have wanted a big sob fest?" Uncle Kurt continued. "If we don't have those people laughing, he'll send down a curse. So just all of you go sit down. I want to go over my material. I'm gonna blow 'em away."

Alice looked at Mary.

"Is your gun loaded?" she said.

13

Mary, Alice, and Jason sat in the front pew. When the priest finished his role in the ceremony, Kurt came on to deliver the eulogy. Mary wanted to shrink down lower, but her knees were already pressed up against the front of the pew.

"We're here to remember Brent Cooper," Uncle Kurt said with a solemn tone to his voice. His head was bowed. He was the absolute picture of somber sincerity. "If anyone's here for the Denny's Early Bird Special – that's two doors down."

Mary closed her eyes and fantasized that she had been adopted. That somewhere her real family was wondering whatever became of that sweet little baby girl they'd put up for adoption.

"The cops are diligently following up every lead," Kurt continued. "And right now, all the leads point in one direction: the Dunkin Donuts on Wilshire."

Behind her, Mary heard one of the old men snoring.

14

This is fantastic.

A tragedy and a farce all rolled into one. I love it! I'd like to get up there and tell everyone how much fun it was to put a bullet into the back of Brent Cooper's finely shaped head. I could improvise a scene: Brent trying to talk St. Peter into admitting him to heaven.

Were his tickets at Will Call?

St. Peter starts to shut the door.

Brent says – Grandma! I came toward the light!

I want to laugh but despite Asshole Kurt Cooper up there, the crowd is deadly – no pun intended – silent. No wonder I'd never seen Kurt. Brent got all the looks and what little humor ran in the Cooper blood.

That girl, though. Mary. She looked like she had something to her.

I've gotta write some of this shit down.

And plan the next one.

15

I n Studio City, among the office buildings and parking
garages put up in the Seventies, sat the condominium
complex for the elderly called Palm Terrace. Like its
residents, the Palm Terrace had seen better days.

Mary parked the Accord in a visitor's spot. She'd gotten
the car out of storage now that the Buick was history. She
went into the office where she found a woman in her fifties
playing online euchre.

"Excuse me," Mary said, after politely waiting the requisite few seconds. The office had cheap paneling and particle
board furniture. It looked like a hospital waiting room. In
Mexico.

The woman held up a finger. She had a heavy sweater,
polyester pants, and gray hair done up in a perm.

"Just one minute," she said. She anxiously watched the
monitor. Mary saw a flutter of movement on the screen and
then the woman shot up from her chair.

"You idiot! Goddamn moron!" She thumped her fist
down on the desk and the keyboard jumped. Mary caught a
glimpse of the screen and saw the card game was over.

"Let me guess – you won," Mary commented.

"Won? How can I win when my own partner, my own *husband*, makes the most boneheaded, infantile moves..."

The woman hit speed dial on her phone and punched the speakerphone button. A man's voice answered.

"Don't start, Rosie..." he said.

"I'm wondering if you have a moment to help me," Mary said, trying to get to the woman before she started in on the phone. But she was too slow.

"How do your internal organs look?" Rosie shouted at the phone. "Huh? That's what you must be looking at since your head is up your ass!" Spittle shot from the woman's mouth and hit the computer monitor. She picked up the phone and slammed it down. Mary heard a dial tone and then nothing.

The woman turned to Mary. "Sorry about that, but we were playing the Jenkinses," the woman said. She lowered her voice. "I can't stand Rhonda Jenkins. The woman is a total bitch. And I absolutely despise losing to her."

"A competitive drive," Mary said. "That's good. So listen, my uncle was murdered," she said. "Brent Cooper?"

The woman's mouth snapped shut. "Oh God, I'm sorry," the woman said.

"Don't worry about it. I just want to see his apartment," Mary said. "Condo. Whatever you call it."

"I'm sorry about that yelling," the woman's face had turned red.

"Hey, don't apologize," Mary said. "You're entitled to enjoy your Golden Years any way you want."

"Tell that to the jackass upstairs," the woman mumbled.

"My uncle's apartment..." Mary said.

The woman shook her head. "The police said I can't let

anyone in. They've been in and out of there a couple times. It's sealed shut."

"I'm sure they didn't mean *everyone*," Mary said. "Family is certainly allowed in."

"Um...I don't know..."

Mary whipped out her p.i. license which she'd put into a slick little leather number that let her flash it like a detective. There was something about a badge that made people more...malleable.

"Not only am I a grieving family member," Mary said. "I'm also working as an adjunct with the police. So you actually *have* to open his condo for me." She wasn't really sure what an adjunct was, but she knew the term was vague enough to avoid any charges of falsely impersonating a cop. But hell, Sergeant Davies did that every day and never got busted.

"Okay, okay. Nothing's more important than family," the woman said. An interesting comment coming from a woman who had just finished verbally abusing her husband, Mary thought.

The woman reached into her desk drawer and pulled out a set of keys. "By the way, my name is..."

"Rosie," Mary said. "Your husband mentioned it when you two were chatting."

"And you are..."

"Mary. Mary Cooper." They shook hands and then Rosie led the way to the elevators. On the wall across from the office a bulletin board held flyers for classes and programs offered to the residents of Palm Terrace. Rosie noticed her looking at the board.

"People think us old folks just sit around and watch the Wheel of Fortune," she said. "That's bull. We write, we paint, we take classes..."

"Any anger management courses up there?" Mary said.

Rosie glanced at her as the elevator doors opened.

"You remind me of Brent," Rosie said.

"No need to get nasty," Mary said.

16

The door was posted with an LAPD notice, but it wasn't sealed. Mary thought it was probably because it wasn't technically a crime scene. In any event, Rosie used her key and opened the door, then followed Mary in.

"Do you mind if I stay?" Rosie said.

Mary did actually mind, but she wasn't about to antagonize Rosie and have her put in a call to the LAPD about a nosy niece. Besides, Mary wanted to keep an eye on Rosie until she was gone.

"Make yourself at home. Throw a fondue party. I don't mind," Mary said.

There wasn't much to see. A small, outdated kitchen. A decent sized living room with a leather couch and beige carpet. There were some posters on the walls, old handbills of comedy shows Uncle Brent had probably been involved in. She couldn't help but feel a little bit of pride for the old man. He may have been abrasive, but he could be pretty damn funny. It pissed her off to see the apartment, see the small amount of success her uncle had experienced. To see how he'd put it on display, and to know that someone had cut his life short. And for what?

Mary followed a short hallway that led to a bathroom and two bedrooms. And that was it. She didn't honestly know what she expected to find. Some letters threatening his life? A diary filled with notes about a person wishing Brent harm?

Mary walked into the main bedroom and took a quick look around. No correspondence. No notes. A few pictures on Brent's dresser. They were mostly black-and-white. Brent as a young man in Hollywood back in the fifties. He'd been really good looking back then, Mary had to admit. His friends all looked like young comics with tans, hip clothes, and money to burn. The few women pictured were lookers, too. Mary recognized a couple of the men in the photographs. One was now a celebrity of sorts, a talk show host. The other was a semi-well-known comic who'd been the brains behind a comedy series.

"Finding anything back there?" Rosie called from the kitchen area.

"Just a bunch of sex toys," Mary called back. "Some of them are pretty heavy duty."

She took a peek in the bathroom. Nothing there but a newspaper in a little shelving unit that held soap and hand towels. It was open to the obituaries, of course. Old people loved to read obituaries. Sort of a sneak preview.

"How much longer do you think you'll be?" Rosie called.

"Sorry, I'm putting some of these sex gadgets into my purse," Mary said. "I'll need to do some very thorough research with them. Lots of testing."

Mary walked back into the living room. "I'm just kidding. I've got all those things at home."

Nothing, Mary thought. I've learned nothing.

"Anything else?" Rosie said, clearly anxious to be done with this.

"I guess not," Mary said.

They left the apartment and Rosie locked the door.

"I suppose you want to talk to the ladies, too? Like the police did?"

Mary stopped. "What ladies?" She looked closely at Rosie and the woman now realized that she'd offered some information that hadn't been requested – always a bad idea.

"Oh, nothing, never mind…"

"Rosie," Mary said. "What ladies?"

She read the expression on the woman's face as realization that it was too late for a retraction. Rosie let out a long, exasperated sigh.

"Apartment 410," she said. "Please don't mention my name. I don't want to get on their bad side."

17

The ladies turned out to be three women in their sixties or up who shared a huge condo. The apartment was tastefully decorated, everything top-of-the-line. Much bigger, much nicer than Brent's place.

Mary thought the women in general looked pretty good for their ages. Their personalities, however, were iffy. The self-appointed spokesperson was Helen, a tall, thin blonde with an attractive but stern face. She had a thin martini glass in her hand, filled with a red concoction. A Cosmo, Mary thought.

Fran was the nervous one. Mary could tell by the way the woman fidgeted on the big white couch. And the way she occasionally bit her lower lip. She was petite and had dark brown hair with frosted tips that probably cost a pretty penny.

The third was the quiet one. Her name was Rachel and she took herself out of the picture quite literally, standing off to the side so Mary had to turn her head to see her. She had black hair and a worn face but a body that Mary would kill for.

"So, what, you're his niece, you said?" the leader, Helen, said.

"That's right," Mary said.

"So what do you want? We told the police everything we knew."

"And what was that? What did you know?"

"Can't you ask the cops for all that?" Helen's voice was deep and stern. This woman could have been an Admiral in the Navy, Mary thought.

"I know this is shocking, but they just don't seem to enjoy sharing everything they know about murder cases with civilians."

The other two women glanced at Helen, as if curious to see how she would react to someone actually standing up to her.

"You don't have to get snippy," Helen said.

"I'm not asking the cops," Mary said, her voice softer but not to the point of pleading. "I'm asking you to help me. Someone murdered my uncle, and I'd like to help find out who. Is there anything you ladies can tell me?"

"Nothing," Helen said. "At least, nothing useful. The cops pretty much told us that."

"Well–" Fran started to say, leaning her head to the side as if she were walking a tightrope, looking for her balance.

"Shut it," Helen snapped. She glared at Fran then turned her gaze back on Mary. She took a sip of her Cosmo and watched Mary over the rim of the glass.

Rachel, who so far hadn't said a word, walked over to the dining room table where a glass pitcher sat, nearly empty. She poured some into a glass, then came over and refilled Helen's. Mary wondered if that entire pitcher had been full and if so, how recently.

"She's probably with the police," Fran whispered to

Helen. She widened her eyes for emphasis. "Maybe she works in the *drug* department."

"Oh, Christ!" Helen shot back. "Why don't you just go play with your vibrator?" Helen then spoke to Mary. "Just ignore her. Look, this is a small community, everyone knows everyone at Palm Terrace. Hell, we could all probably show the cops a thing or two when it comes to surveillance. But we really don't know anything."

Fran got up and paced behind the couch. Mary watched her and thought, *Come on, crack, Fran. Crack.*

"So why did the police talk to just you three?" Mary said. She had no idea if that was true, that they hadn't questioned anyone else at the building, but if she was wrong the ladies would correct her.

They didn't.

Mary put the thousand-yard stare on Fran, the weak link.

Helen drained the last of her Cosmo in one long swallow. She started to speak but then Mary saw a shudder run through Fran's body. Fran wheeled on Mary.

"It's our fault!" she said.

Helen slammed down her glass and jumped to her feet. "Goddamnit!"

"I can't survive in prison!" Fran shouted back. "Do you know what those big nasty guards would do? I've got a nice ass! They'd be all over me trying to..."

"...trying to get you to shut the hell up!" Helen shouted.

"Are you with the drug people? The AFT? The ATM? What are they called?" Fran asked Mary.

"No, I'm not with the police or the government. But I do like drugs. All kinds really," Mary said. "I sniffed a bunch of glue on my way over here, actually."

Now the quiet one, Rachel, spoke up. "Hah! She's a

smart-ass, just like Brent!"

"I'm just going to come out and say it," Fran said.

"Here she goes..." Helen said, shrugging her shoulders and walking toward the kitchen.

"We illegally..." Fran started to say.

"Hit me," Helen said to Rachel, who had put together a fresh pitcher of Cosmos and now dutifully refilled Helen's glass.

"...filled Viagra prescriptions," Fran finished.

Mary closed her eyes. She hadn't really been expecting these ladies to confess to her uncle's murder, but still. Viagra?

"Are you going to arrest us?" Fran said.

"They were for my uncle, weren't they?" Mary said. "That's why the police talked to you?"

"We were his harem," Helen offered. Apparently, now that Fran had dumped the goods out for all to see, she had thrown in the towel, too.

"Okay?" Helen said. "We all took turns. We shared him. But it started to get to be too much for him. And we were at each other's throats because say, if Rachel did Brent in the afternoon, he couldn't get hard for me in the evening..."

"Please..." Mary started to say.

"...he'd be a goddamn limp noodle for me," Helen said, glaring at Rachel.

"We had his schlong on timeshare," Fran said, her nervous energy rapidly changing into giddy relief.

"And his balls, too," Rachel said, her words now slightly slurring.

"He had a nice tool," Helen said, a wistful note in her voice.

"And he sure knew how to use it," Rachel said.

"Ladies!" Mary said. "I don't need the details. I really

don't."

"So we had to come up with a system for Viagra," Helen continued. "Because his prescription wasn't enough. So we got another guy here to have his doctor prescribe it, then we reimbursed him, plus we'd give him a little something extra for his effort."

"But you didn't have anything to do with his murder," Mary said.

"Not unless you count trying to screw him to death," Rachel said. Both Helen and Fran giggled.

"Not unless you count sitting on his face and trying to smother him," Rachel said, on a roll.

"Stop, okay?"

The ladies were barely able to stifle their giggles.

"No, I don't believe any of that would hold up in court as attempted murder," Mary said. "Did you have anything else to offer the police?"

"Just the last time we saw him, which was Rachel," Helen said.

"Well, technically," Rachel said. "I didn't see him because he was behind me the whole time." Rachel thrust her hips forward and made an ass-slapping motion with her hand.

"Why do I feel like I'm in a locker room?" Mary said.

"When we did it doggy, he used to do this trick..."

"With his thumb, right?" Fran said.

"Thank you, ladies!" Mary pulled out her card. "Call me if you think of anything not involving details of my deceased uncle's genitalia."

"We're always here to help," Helen said with a straight face. "But we've got nothing else to tell you."

Mary opened the door.

"Come back anytime, Mary!" Fran called out.

18

"Y ou sure that's all you want, baby? Information?"

Mary leaned against the door frame of the dressing room, if you could call it that, behind the stage at the Leg Pull. Cecil, the manager, hadn't lied to her about when the comedian who might know the identity of Brent's 'friend' would be performing.

She looked at Jimmy Miles, a fifty-ish black guy wearing a glittery shirt and shiny black pants. A half a bottle of Jheri Curl had to be in his hair.

"Liberace know you're wearing his shirt?" she said.

She had come directly from her office where she'd tied up some loose ends on another case, filed paperwork, and cleared her e-mail. She'd also tried to erase from her memory banks the X-rated information she'd received from the three Senior Nymphs at Palm Terrace. It wasn't an easy thing to do.

After she left the office she came over once more to the Leg Pull to try to find out more information about Uncle Brent's partner. When she pulled up to the place, she vowed that once Brent's killer was locked up or dead, Mary would never come anywhere near the Leg Pull again.

Now, the Liberace comment had hit home and Jimmy's eyes went wide in feigned shock. "Whooooeee!" he said. "That is some kinda mouth you got. Naughty, naughty, naughty."

"Naughty? Let me guess, now you're going to ask me if I need a spanking. Come on, if you're not funny, try at least to be original."

The comedian gave her a big smile. "You sure are quick, baby! I like that!"

"I really appreciate that, Jimmy. High praise," Mary said. "Now I'd like to make this quick, too. Brent Cooper."

Jimmy's eyes went wide again. "That guy got killed out back? What about him? Not me – I'm a lover not a fighter."

"You know anything about the guy he was performing with that night?" Mary said. "Your boss Cecil said you knew everyone."

"Shit."

"According to Cecil, you're a regular gossip hound."

"Who does he think he is labeling me like that?" His voice had risen a couple of octaves. "No one labels me! Goddamn, I'd like to kick his ass one of these days."

"Ease up there, Macho Man."

"You makin' fun of me?"

"No, I'm being sincere. Just tell me who he is or where he is, I don't care which."

Jimmy looked at her. "You like my shirt?"

Mary debated about pulling out the .45 again, but decided against it. So she said, "I love your shirt. I'll stop by Radio City Music Hall and ask the Rockettes if I can borrow one of theirs so we can match."

"That's how it's gonna be, huh?" he said. "Tell you what.

Ordinarily I'd let a pretty little lady like you buy me a couple drinks first. But since I go on in about ten minutes, I don't think I should be partaking in any of that nice booze out there. So why don't you just give me some of that cash riding on that sweet ass of yours and I'll buy myself a couple shots after the show. I'll even toast you. That's how Jimmy rolls, baby."

Mary sighed and pulled out a twenty. She held it in the air.

"Let me hear something other than all those crackling sequins," she said.

Jimmy snorted. "Asshole's name is Barry Olis," he said. "Some old, un-funny geezer lives over at the Vista Del Mar apartments on Venice. Only reason I know that is because he's got some lame-ass joke in his routine about it."

Mary gave him the twenty.

"Add that to your wardrobe budget."

19

V ista del Mar. View of the ocean, or Oceanview, in Spanish. Not quite, Mary thought. More like Vista del Winos and Liquor Stores.

She parked the Accord and went to the apartment complex's lobby, if you could call it that. It was more like a combination phone booth and port-a-potty. Small, dirty, and home to a few mystery puddles that looked like Apple Pucker after it'd been processed through someone's over-sized liver.

Jeez, Mary thought. Uncle Brent's place was like Camelot compared to this shithole.

She was surprised to see the name Olis listed on one of the mailbox slots. #312. Mary looked around but didn't see an elevator so she took the stairs. On the first landing, a man lay sprawled in his own vomit.

"That's okay, don't get up," Mary said as she passed him by. The man moaned and gargled at the same time. The smell made Mary hold her breath until she reached the third floor.

As Mary opened the door and began walking down the

hallway toward 312, she thought about Barry Olis. The name didn't ring any kind of bell with her, but this was Hollywood. Uncle Brent had met and known untold numbers of people as a comedian and writer. There were probably hundreds of names she'd never heard of. Mary wondered if Uncle Brent had known this Barry guy recently or if they were old friends. Hopefully, Barry had seen something that had happened the night Brent was murdered. As of right now, there still weren't any real witnesses.

Mary finally came to Apartment 312. Farther down the hall, she heard a door slam and someone shout. She put her right hand inside her sport coat on the butt of her .45. With her left hand, she reached up and knocked.

The door gave a little under her knock, and she saw that not only was the door unlocked, it wasn't even latched shut. She looked both ways down the hall before taking her .45 all the way out of her shoulder holster. "Hello?" she said. "Anyone home?"

Again with her left hand she reached up and gave a very gentle knock. The door creaked inward and in a flash, Mary saw the thin wire stretched across the opening and she dove to her left as a bright flash blinded her and then a tremendous roar filled her ears. She felt herself lifted off the floor and then smashed into something hard.

For just a moment, she wondered if she looked just like the guy passed out in the stairwell.

And then she didn't wonder anymore.

20

"I always knew I'd see you in bed again soon."

Mary opened her eyes, despite the crushing headache that made her grind her jaws. She was on a rolling bed in an ambulance, parked outside the Vista del Mar. Jake Cornell looked down at her, a look of bemusement on his face. It made her head hurt even worse.

"And I knew you'd have to knock me unconscious to do it," she said. Ooh, it hurt to talk, too. She ran a quick inventory up and down her body and discovered that just about everything ached.

"The blast knocked you backward and you hit your head on the fire extinguisher hanging on the wall," Jake said. "You were lucky. It could have been a fire axe instead."

Mary thought of a couple comebacks, but it hurt too much to actually say them. She groaned and struggled to sit up. The pain actually lessened once she was up, but now she felt sore ribs, too. When she looked up, what she saw next really hurt.

Sergeant Arianna Davies now stood next to Jake. The Shark apparently smelled blood.

Mary turned to the paramedic who was next to her, closing up his medical kit. "Do you have anything in there that will make her go away?" she said, nodding toward the Shark. The paramedic pretended not to hear her.

"You really don't want to keep your p.i. license do you, Cooper?" Davies said. "I told you to stay away from this case."

"Well, maybe you should sign me up for the same obedience course you put him through," Mary said, nodding toward Jake.

"Why were you here, Mary?" Jake asked. He tried to put it gently, but Mary still hated him for asking anyway. Traitor.

"Deadbeat Dad case I'm working on," she said. "Supposedly the guy was hiding out here. Turns out he has a psychotic daughter." She turned to Davies. "Your Mom hired me to find him."

"Not funny," Davies said.

"In Apartment 312?" Jake asked.

"Deadbeat Dads don't put their names on their mailboxes, Jake. You'll learn that when you become a detective." Jake's face flashed red, and for a moment, Mary felt bad, which surprised her. She didn't want to hurt him, just sting him a little. And she really didn't want to ruin his career.

"Ever heard of a man named Barrymore Olis?" Davies said. "Barry Olis to his friends?"

"I know an Oily Boris, but not a Barry Olis."

"Well, there was a body in 312, and the apartment belonged to a Barry Olis," Davies said.

"Excellent deduction, detective," Mary said.

Jake pulled out a sheet of paper. "Any idea what this means?" But before Mary could answer, the Shark snatched the paper from Jake's hand.

"Let's *get* information, Detective Cornell," Davies said. A hard edge to her voice that perfectly complemented her entire being. "Not *give* it. We're all done here," she said. The Shark turned her full attention on Mary. "Stay away from me, Cooper. This is your last warning."

The Shark stormed off with Jake in tow.

But it didn't matter. Mary didn't really care what the Shark threatened to do. She'd gotten a good look at that sheet of paper in Jake's hand. A part of her wanted to believe that Jake had done it on purpose, to give her the information but make it look like he'd done it accidentally. Her heart lightened a little bit and she almost smiled.

Mary had seen that piece of paper, and she had read it. So she knew what she had to do.

It had been three little words. But words that tied this murder into Uncle Brent's.

The note had been in big block letters.

He really bombed.

21

"I always knew your career choice would blow up in your face," Aunt Alice said as she let Mary inside the house. Mary rolled her eyes. A man in a pair of black slacks and a black turtleneck rose from the couch to greet her.

"This is Whitney Braggs," Alice said. "Whitney, this is my niece, Kojak."

"Mary, actually."

"Nice to meet you Mary Actually."

Oh God, Mary thought. Everyone's a comedian. Braggs smiled at her and Mary noted the brilliant white teeth, the smooth, tanned skin and the perfect white hair. This guy was probably in his late sixties, but he clearly took good care of himself.

"Really, though," he said. "I know you're a Cooper. Brent and I went way back. I'm sorry for your loss." His voice was smooth and cultured. He sounded like a radio announcer.

"Mary, can I get you anything?" Alice said. "A drink of water? An application to a local community college?"

Mary had been released several hours ago. The prognosis had been good. No broken bones. A slight concussion, most likely. Right now, she just felt sore and tired.

"Ladies," Braggs said. "Since you're both slightly inca- pacitated, allow me." He escorted Alice to a chair. Even though she was walking now, it wasn't a very steady gait. Mary didn't bother waiting for him. She sat down on the yellow chair next to Alice. Alice asked for iced tea and Mary asked for a Diet Coke. Mary caught a waft of subtle, expen- sive cologne.

Once Braggs had left for the kitchen, Mary turned to Aunt Alice. "So is the sex good with him?"

Alice looked at her out of the corner of her eye and answered in a soft voice.

"Why, would you be jealous?" she said.

"Looks like you didn't even ruffle his hair."

"He got so excited there wasn't time…"

The return of Braggs with the drinks cut Alice off.

"Whitney says that a group of Brent's friends are all coming to town," Alice offered.

"There go our property values," Mary said. "Buy your polyester shirts and Sansabelts now, before they're gone."

"Some of them are actually here, living here," Braggs said. "But yeah, there are a few out-of-towners. You know, we were all pretty close back in the day," he said, his face thoughtful. Mary thought he was a pretty good actor, too.

"When you say 'we', who are you talking about?" she asked.

"She's a p.i.," Alice said. "She asks questions all the time. Let me know if she starts bugging you, I've got a muzzle for her, it has her monogram on it…"

"Yeah," Mary said. "And I've got her ball gag in my purse."

"No, no, no," Braggs said. "That's fine, that's fine," he

said, holding out his finely manicured hands. Jeez, Mary thought. The guy's got better nails than I do.

"Just some friends who all started together way back when," he said. "We sort of cheered each other on, critiqued each other's jokes. If one of us got a job, he'd try to get some of us hired, too, or at least submit our material."

"So you guys were all comedians, or what?" Mary said.

"Most of us did stand-up. All of us wrote material, too, and tried to get jobs on TV. shows. You know, talk shows, variety shows, sitcoms. Some of us did, some of us didn't."

"Did you?" Alice asked.

"I had some early success," he said. His expression was one of careful modesty. "A few little roles on the Dick Van Dyke Show, and others. But then I went into commercial voiceover work." He smiled. "Visa. The only card you need."

"Yes, that's you! I thought I recognized your voice. That's impressive!" Alice said.

"So are the royalty checks," Braggs said with a wink.

"Sorry about my last payment," Alice said. "I swear I mailed it out in time, but the frickin' mail is so slow!"

"I heard her say the same thing to the cable guy," Mary said. "Let me ask you something, Mr. Braggs."

"Please, Whitney."

"Did you ever know a Barry Olis?"

"Yes! I knew Barry," Braggs said, surprise in his voice. "I tried to track him down, too, but couldn't find an address."

"Well, he's now in multiple locations," Mary said. Alice and Braggs gave her a blank look.

"He was in the apartment that exploded," she said. "The one that nearly took me with it."

"Oh, dear God," Braggs said. Mary noted that his face went slightly pale. Although, with his tan, it was more like it went slightly taupe.

"Do they know who did it?" he asked.

"They know the killer has a really good sense of humor," Mary said.

"What do you mean?" he asked.

She shook her head. "Nothing, it's not important." Mary then thought of something. She gestured to both Aunt Alice and Braggs. "So did you two know each other? Why did you come here, to her place? To see what happens to upholstery gone bad?"

"I knew Brent had a sister in town, he'd mentioned that," Braggs said. "A few phone calls and I found the particulars. I missed the funeral."

"Too bad, it was a good show," Mary said. "A regular laugh fest."

"Coopers just can't be serious about anything," Alice said. "Especially her," she said, then lifted a cane and pointed it at Mary.

"So do the police think Brent's and Barry Olis' murders are connected?" Braggs asked.

"I'm not exactly the person they like to share intimate details with," Mary said. "In fact, they keep warning me they'll take my license away. I think they feel threatened."

"Do they know it's a cosmetician's license?" Alice said.

"Okay," Braggs said. "Then let me ask you this, Mary. Do you think the murders are connected?"

"They're tied together more tightly than Alice's black lace bodystocking."

"It's not black, it's fire-engine red, baby," Alice said, a small smile tugging at the corner of her mouth.

"Oh, boy. This is serious," Braggs said, resting his chin in his hand and looking out Alice's picture window. There wasn't much to see out there, Mary thought. A few houses.

Not a whole lot of inspiration. Nonetheless, Braggs sat straight up and clapped his hands together.

"Brent also mentioned you," he said to Mary.

"I'm sure it was a real Hallmark moment," Mary said.

Braggs smiled an easy, comforting smile. "He simply mentioned he had a niece who was a helluva private investigator. I swear, that's what he said."

"He was probably joking, testing out some new material," Alice offered.

"Well, that's kind of why I came to see Alice," Braggs said.

"You need a good reason. No one would do it on their own volition," Mary said.

"I came here to see Alice, but I also came to find you," he said.

"Visiting Mary is like rubbernecking at a car accident – you don't really want to, but sometimes you just can't stop yourself."

"Why me?" Mary said.

"The group of guys I told you about? The ones who all started out with Brent and me way back when?"

Mary nodded.

"We want to hire you to find Brent's killer," Braggs said. "And now Barry's too."

Her first inclination was to say absolutely not. But she was looking into the case anyway, so she may as well get paid for it. Plus, since she had a legitimate client now, she actually had a legal right to do some investigating. At least, enough right to challenge the Shark the next time they butted heads.

"There's only one condition," Braggs said.

Uh-oh, Mary thought.

"I'm coming with you."

22

M ary shot up Pico, then hooked a left onto Lincoln. A few minutes later she pulled up in front of the Leg Pull. Mary hoped once and for all that this would be the last time she had to come to this shithole.

But then she smiled and laughed about Mr. Whitney Braggs. Thinking he could tag along just because he'd hired her. What was she, a ride share program for the elderly? That's why she had slipped out the back door of Aunt Alice's house. She didn't have time to babysit some old man.

She eased out of the car, her body still ached. Mary dry swallowed some more Tylenol.

She walked into the Leg Pull and saw her good friend Mr.

Cecil Fogerty, standing at the bar, watching the bartender, a very well-endowed young woman. Mary figured the woman would last about a week, or at least until Cecil started putting the moves on her and she slapped him silly. At least, hopefully that's what she would do, for her own sake.

Fogerty glanced out the corner of his eye when she walked in, stiffened as if someone had shoved a cattle prod up his ass, then immediately turned his back on her. Mary walked right up to him.

"Hey Cecil! Long time no see!" she said.

He turned to look at her over his shoulder. The bartender moved on so Cecil had no choice but to turn all the way around and face her.

"I told you everything I know," he said.

"Ah, come on," Mary said. "You went to MIT right? You must be a real fountain of knowledge."

"Please go away," he said, his voice small and sheepish.

"I can't stay away from you," Mary said. "I'm hooked. It's like asking a bird not to fly."

"You know," he said, the light of a small challenge coming into his eyes. "I reported you to the cops for pulling your gun on me," he said. He even puffed out his chest a little.

"No you didn't," Mary said just as loud. "You changed your soaked panties and told everyone you did me on the desk."

"Yeah, but after that, I called the cops."

Mary could tell he was lying. He wouldn't dare call the cops and get involved with them. She was sure Cecil had all kinds of sideline activities the police would love to know about. And she didn't have time to listen to his bullshit. Mary closed the distance on him and stood so close her boobs were hitting him in his chest. She could smell his body odor mixed with some high-octane Hai Karate. Mary tried not to look at the greasy pores on the man's nose.

"Jimmy Miles," she said. "Where is he?"

"Here we go again," Cecil said. His voice actually shook a little and his chest caved back in.

"Is that your breath or are we standing over an open sewer?" Mary said.

Cecil gritted his teeth. "I have very active glands," he said. "It's not fair of you to make fun of something I can't control."

Mary reached up and grabbed the front of Fogerty's shirt. The bartender looked over as well as a cocktail waitress who had reappeared from the back room.

"Tell me," Mary said.

"I don't know," Fogerty said through clenched, yellowed teeth. "Go look in one of those Comedy Club flyers – it shows where everyone is. He's probably listed in there."

Mary nodded. "That's a good idea. But since you know the clubs, you could probably find it much faster than I could. Go."

She pushed him away from the bar.

"Then will you leave and never come back?" Fogerty said, and walked over to the pile of thin newspapers. He picked one up, then mumbled under his breath. "Maybe go get some horrible disease and die a miserable death?"

"Stop trying to sweet talk me," Mary said.

He flipped through the pages, scanning them quickly. Mary took a look around. The place was mostly empty. She pictured her Uncle Brent here, waiting to go on stage for his final performance. She hoped he had gotten at least a few laughs.

"Donny B's," Fogerty said. "On Sunset in West Hollywood. Okay?"

"Even though I trust you implicitly, show me," Mary said. Fogerty held open the paper and Mary saw Jimmy Miles' name in the rectangle for Donny B's. She took the paper and headed for the door.

"Please don't come back," Fogerty said.

"Don't wait up for me, honey," Mary answered.

23

Mary had figured the Leg Pull was at the bottom rung of the comedy club ladder.

She was wrong.

Donny B's was under the ladder, down a manhole cover, on par with the sewer lines. Small, dirty, and nearly empty, Donny B's looked less like a comedy club and more like a dive biker bar even hobos would be embarrassed to frequent.

Jimmy Miles was on stage. Mary checked her watch. According to the flyer he was most likely in the middle of his set. She sat at the bar and ordered a beer. In a bottle. She swiveled on her stool and took in Jimmy's act.

"And you know what else I love about black women?" he said. All nervous energy on the stage. "It's okay to insult them. Just don't do it in their house!" He waved his finger in front of him and raised his voice up a pitch or two. "You gonna say that to me *in my house*? You got another thing comin, girl!" There was chuckle or two from the audience, Mary thought. Well, just one.

"So I can call you a ho' as long as I stand on the front

steps and don't actually come *in the house*?" Jimmy said. This time, he was met with dead silence.

Mary turned away from the carnage and took a drink of her beer. She thought about what had happened. Uncle Brent murdered. Barry Olis murdered. One attempt on her life. And a message conveyed by somebody shooting up her Buick.

Robbery certainly wasn't a motive. The only drugs involved were Viagra. So why the hell would somebody want to murder a couple of washed up comedians? It made no sense. Was the killer just after the Coopers? Did Barry Olis become a collateral victim? Mary went through the case again but there was nothing. Nothing she'd missed anyway. But you never knew. You had to just keep plugging away.

Mary took another pull of her beer and glanced up as a smattering of applause broke out. Jimmy Miles stepped off the stage, wiping his sopping wet face. Nothing makes you sweat like dying on stage, Mary thought.

Jimmy headed straight for her. How could he not, she thought. She stuck out of the crowd so badly, she might as well have been phosphorescent.

"So now you're going to buy me that drink, baby?" Jimmy said, and plopped onto the bar stool next to her.

"Sure, what the hell," Mary said. "You must be thirsty after all that hilarity."

"Yeah, I remember you," he said. "The one that's always got something to say." The bartender set a beer in front of Jimmy.

"Here's to silence," Mary said and clinked Jimmy's bottle.

She watched him drain half the beer in three big swallows. "So now that I've bought you a drink," she said. "Why don't you tell me who paid you to send me off to Vista del Mar?" she said. Mary watched his reaction closely and recognized the briefest flash of surprise in his eyes. He recovered quickly.

"Hell no!" he said. "Nobody told me to send you over there! You one of them conspiracy theory people? Aliens landed and shot Kennedy?"

"Ah, the beauty of true words being spoken."

"Don't give me that shit," he said. "I'm serious. That old dude told me where he lived, like he wanted me to come over and grill some hot dogs with him or somethin'. Maybe he's into handsome black dudes. Can you blame the poor bastard? Shit."

Mary let it all go by. "Now, Jimmy. I hate to point out your blatant lies..."

"Hush your mouth!" he said.

"...but the first time I asked you where the old guy lived you told me it was part of his act," she said. "You said that's how you knew where he lived. Remember?"

"No."

"Now you're telling me something different. That this old guy told you where he lived, as opposed to it being part of his act. So which one is it? Which one is the truth?"

"I hate to disappoint a pretty lady," he said. "But you're barking up the wrong tree, baby." He took a long drink from his beer and set it back down on the bar, empty. He stood up to go.

Suddenly, a deep, cultured voice behind Mary spoke. "Why don't you tell the woman what she wants to know?"

Mary turned into the face of Whitney Braggs.

"Oh, Christ," she said.

"More like Moses without the beard," Jimmy said.

"Shut up, punk," Braggs said to Jimmy. To Mary, it was incredibly odd to hear such coarseness come from a man who looked like a spokesman for the AARP.

"Who the hell are you?" Miles said. "Bob friggin' Barker? Why don't you go back to the Price is Right? Or if not that, the goddamned nursing home!"

Braggs walked past Mary and to Jimmy's other side. He looked at the bartender. "I'll have what they're having."

When the bartender turned to get the beer, Braggs slammed his forehead into Jimmy's face.

"Shit!" Mary said.

She heard the crunch of cartilage. Jimmy sagged but Braggs held him aloft and half-walked, half-dragged him to the door.

"I don't believe this," Mary said as she threw some bills onto the bar.

She stepped outside just as Braggs propped Jimmy up against the wall. With lightning fast speed, Braggs hit him twice in the belly, then threw a wicked uppercut that made Jimmy's head snap back into the brick wall. Another right and another left drove into Jimmy's face. Blood covered the comedian's face. Teeth dropped onto the sidewalk.

"Stop it," Mary said, stepping toward Braggs. Braggs ignored her and grabbed a handful of Jimmy's greasy hair and held him upright against the wall.

"Who told you to lie, asshole?" he shouted. "Who got to you? I need a name. Right here. Right now."

Mary reached inside her coat and reached for her .45.

"Braggs, you are going to let him go right now," she said.

Just as her automatic cleared leather, Jimmy coughed and spat out blood.

"No name," he said.

"Liar."

"Sheet of paper," Jimmy gasped. "Two hundred bucks if I did it. Bad news if I didn't. What did I care?"

"So you never knew Barry Olis?" Mary asked, keeping the .45 inside its holster for the moment.

"Shit no!"

"You don't know anyone," Braggs said, sneering. "How convenient. You worthless shit!"

"Shut up Braggs," Mary said.

"Matter of fact, I don't!" Jimmy said. "I don't know no names. But I do know something else."

"Yeah?" Braggs said, his voice dripping with doubt.

"Yeah," Jimmy said. "I know who killed Brent Cooper."

24

"He was a big guy," Jimmy said, and spat out more blood and another tooth.

"Did you see the actual murder?" Mary asked.

"Nah, but..."

"Then how do you know who did it?" Braggs said.

"Cuz he and Cooper were really goin' at it, man."

"What do you mean going at it?" Mary said. She heard the sound of sirens in the distance and shot a look at Braggs. "You mean like fighting?" she said to Jimmy. "In the alley?"

"During Cooper's act, man. The guy was hecklin' him somethin' fierce."

"A heckler killed him?" Braggs said. "Yeah, right. You can do better than that, jerkwad."

"But Cooper, man. That guy had a nasty mouth. Almost as bad as yours," Jimmy said, looking at Mary. "Cooper ripped that guy a new one. The dude was huge and Cooper went off on all these fat jokes. Christ, he had a million of 'em. The guy couldn't take it and finally left, the few people there was all laughin' at him."

"How come you didn't tell the cops any of this?" Braggs said.

Mary looked at Braggs. How the hell could he know what was told to the cops and what wasn't?

"No one asked," Miles said. "'Cept her," he said, again looking at Mary.

"Do you know the big guy's name?" Mary said.

"Nuh-uh," Jimmy said. "But he's a regular at all the comedy clubs. You can't miss him. Sometimes he likes the attention, you know. Some of the guys like to make fat jokes about him and he don't mind. Sorta likes the attention. But Cooper, man. He just *went off* on him."

"What's he look like? Other than being a big guy," Mary said.

"Tall, too. Maybe 6'4", 6'5". Gotta be 350, 400 pounds, easy. Usually wears a suit and tie and a baseball cap."

The sirens were closer and Mary looked at Braggs. "Give him something for the abuse."

"What do you mean?" Braggs said.

"She means cash, Lawrence Welk! 'Less you want me to go tell the cops how you and your girlfriend here assaulted me. What are you," he said to Mary. "One of Barker's Beauties?"

"Shut up, Jimmy," Mary said.

Braggs whipped out his wallet and was carefully selecting a bill. Mary reached in, grabbed a handful of fifties and shoved them into Jimmy's shirt pocket.

"Hey..." Braggs said.

"What are you worried about?" Mary said. "Bill it to Visa."

"Visa?" Jimmy said. "I thought I recognized that voice. You the Visa dude?"

Jimmy looked at Mary, then back to Braggs, then down the front of his shirt which was streaked with blood.

"Always hated those commercials."

25

M ary pulled the Accord into the parking lot of Chez Jay's, a dive bar on Ocean with a legendary pedigree. Now, it was mostly made up of tourists and business people from one of the many hotels across the street. The occasional star popped in, when they decided to go slumming.

She had told Braggs to meet her here as they both hurried to their cars, away from Jimmy bloody Miles and the encroaching sirens.

Mary shut the car off and thought about what Braggs had done. It had worked, she had gotten a good lead, but still. That strong-arm bullshit rarely worked. It typically got you a couple nights in jail, and if you were a p.i., a fond farewell to your license.

Headlights splashed across the painted mural on the cinderblock wall of Chez Jay's. It was some kind of mermaid riding a wave.

Mary glanced over and saw Braggs behind the wheel of a sleek black Bentley 8, the two-door coupe that everyone who was anyone now drove in L.A. Mary shook her head. Figures. The sick thing was, Braggs fit the car perfectly.

She chastised herself. How could she not have seen Braggs tailing her from Aunt Alice's to Donny B's? That was sloppy and amateurish. The words made her grind her teeth. She got out and leaned against the back of her Accord. Braggs stepped out, set the alarm on the Bentley, and walked over to her.

"I always liked this place. Did you ever hear that story about Steve McQueen..."

Mary stepped in front of him.

"I want you to close your Visa sounding piehole," Mary said. "And listen to me."

Braggs raised a perfectly manicured eyebrow.

"You will not follow me again," she said. "You will not continue any active role in this investigation. You are my client. Not my partner. If you further impede my inquiries I will cease our business relationship and keep your retainer. And somewhere in there I may have to kick your liver-spotted ass."

Braggs smirked at her. "I don't think 'impede' is an accurate depiction of my contributions to the investigation thus far..."

"This is not open for debate."

"Augment. Enhance. Improve," Braggs said, ignoring her. "Those would be far better descriptors of my role..."

"Jackass would be a far better descriptor of you..."

Braggs held up one of his beautifully manicured hands. Mary guessed that he'd carefully wiped the blood off before he'd gotten into his car. Probably with a silk handkerchief.

"Say no more, Ms. Cooper. I shall inconspicuously retreat into the scenery."

Mary shook her head. He sounded like a Shakespearean

trained actor. A few minutes back, he sounded like some nasty cop from Serpico.

Mary turned and got back into her car.

As she was about to back out, Braggs rapped lightly on her window. She rolled it down.

"Are you sure you don't want to have a drink?"

"Nah," Mary said. "This place is for has-beens."

26

Mary did want a drink, she just didn't want to have one with Braggs, Mr. Dual Personality. She wondered, did Visa realize the voice of their company was a complete psycho?

All she really wanted to do was relax in front of her fireplace and have some wine. Mary stopped at a little market a block or so from her condo. They had a good selection of wine and the only drawback was Julia Roberts always went there for this or that, so that meant there were always a few people going for a look at Julia Roberts. But despite the sometimes long lines, she loved their oddball selection. She picked out a chardonnay and a pinot grigio, then went back to her condo.

She was just getting her keys out when the door of the condo next to her opened. Mary was surprised. It had been vacant since about four months before when a young character actor she'd met once or twice had died of an overdose.

A man stepped out into the hall. He had on a tan sport coat with jeans and tan leather shoes. He looked up at Mary and smiled.

"Hello," he said.

"Hi," Mary said back, momentarily caught off guard by how handsome he was. Really bright blue eyes and wavy light brown hair. Nice build. She stopped in front of her door.

"Do you live here?" the man said.

"I wish. I'm actually the plumber," Mary said. She nodded her head toward her own door. "Their toilet's backed up again." She hefted the bottle of Chardonnay. "I use this instead of Drano."

The guy raised his eyebrows, a slight smile on his face. He knew she was kidding around. Hmm, the guy was quick. She liked that.

She smiled. "Mary Cooper," she said and stuck out her hand.

He shook her hand. "Chris McAllister," he said.

Mary liked his handshake. It was warm, not too strong, not too weak.

"I'm moving in, just got the keys this morning," he said. "Do you like it here?" he said.

"I do, especially because it's close to my liquor supply."

He laughed then, a soft easy smile that showed his perfect white teeth.

"Well," he said. "I'm going to finish bringing this stuff up. It was nice to meet you, Mary."

"Nice to meet you, too," she said. She stepped inside her apartment and closed the door behind her, then leaned her back against it. Whoa, she thought. It wasn't that she didn't see many handsome guys. There were plenty of them in L.A. Jake Cornell being one of them. Plus, a lot of her clients were in the entertainment industry, Home Central for the Hotties. But there was something different about this Chris guy.

Mary walked to the kitchen and got the wine opener. She twisted it, cranked it downward into the cork, then clamped down and slowly drew it out of the bottle. She liked her chardonnay slightly chilled, but didn't feel like waiting now. Patience was overrated and instant gratification was just plain getting a bad rap.

She went to her stereo, run by her iPod, and put on some Jamie Cullum, the young British jazz sensation and her favorite artist of late. You couldn't get a ticket in London to see him, but in the States, fourteen bucks got you front row seats.

She settled into her couch, put her feet up, and looked out her picture window at the dark ocean.

The chardonnay hit the spot. She thought about what Braggs had done to Jimmy Miles. That had been bad.

Mary got up and rummaged around the fridge for something to eat. The wine had gone straight to her head. She'd been popping Tylenol, still hurting a bit from the bomb blast.

Finally, she dug out a plastic bowl filled with some hazelnut pesto pasta that she'd made a couple days ago. She grabbed a fork and sat at the kitchen table, looking out past the living room toward the water.

For the millionth time, Mary wondered why she had insisted on a condo with a view of the ocean. Her parents had died in the Pacific when she was just three. Lost during a storm while sailing their 36' catamaran. The bodies had never been found. It was right after that she'd moved in with Aunt Alice, who had raised her.

Mary toyed with the pasta but she'd lost her appetite. She threw it away then filled her glass again.

Her mind drafted back to her new neighbor. It had been awhile since her last relationship.

A lot of the guys she'd been with had two big problems with her: one, she was a little bit sarcastic. And two, she carried a gun and knew how to use it. A lot of times, guys were okay with one of those. It was the rare individual who could handle both.

The comedy club names were a parade of bad puns: Punch's Line. The Delivery Room. Stand Me Up.

Mary went to them all. She talked to every bartender, manager, and comedian she could find. She sat and listened to countless comedians talk about such lofty topics as why women check their makeup in the mirror, why there's so much meat on pizza, and observations on the differences between New York City and Los Angeles. She wondered why so many had the same material. Maybe that's why they were in these shithole comedy clubs instead of on the Tonight Show.

It was at the Comedy Cabin, designed like a log cabin in the Adirondacks, that Mary found the first glimmer of recognition.

"Yeah, I've seen him," the bartender said. He was a skinny white guy with a soul patch and a black T-shirt. "Dickbag never tips. I love it when someone rips him a new one. He deserves it."

"Is 'Dickbag' his Christian name, or does he go by something else?" Mary said.

"No clue, babe. All I know is he's stupid and obnoxious. And he's got a thing for a chick comic. The one who wears the leather pants all the time?"

He looked at Mary as if she could spout out the name immediately. "No clue, babe," she said back to him.

"Ask Janet. She's a scout for one of the networks or something. She knows everyone." He lifted his chin toward an older woman with big red hair, thick black glasses, and sagging skin.

Mary went over to her. "Excuse me," Mary said.

"Head shot with credits. Leave it on the table," the woman said. Her voice raspy and bored.

"Thanks for your obvious interest," Mary said. "But I'm not looking to get hired."

"Then go away. You're interrupting Mr. Jenkins' hilarious take on airline food," the woman said, referring to the disheveled comic on stage. "Turns out, the food's not very good. Imagine that."

Mary pulled out a chair and sat down next to the woman. "Thanks for the invite," she said. "Get you another martini or will that affect your lovely personality?"

"Sure," the woman said. "I'll take another martini and while I'm drinking it, you can place your lips directly on my buttocks. How's that?"

"Yum, very tempting," Mary said. She waved to the waitress and gestured for a refill on the old lady's drink.

"My name's Mary Cooper and I'm looking for a female comic, wears leather pants all the time."

"What, you got the hots for her?"

Jesus, Mary thought. What was the deal with these old people? Do they just get nastier with age?

"Absolutely," Mary said. "Never met a woman I didn't like. Until now."

"I'm Janet Venuta and you're a smart ass. I like that. Now go to hell." She reached for the fresh martini with greed in her eyes. "And thanks for the drink."

The old woman took a long, loud slurp from her martini.

"Gosh," Mary pointed out. "You just could not be any more likeable."

"True," the woman said. "Bye bye now. Go away."

"The guy behind the bar said you know everyone in these clubs," Mary said, ignoring her last directive. "And I'm sick and tired of going into these shitholes meeting the dregs of society. Yourself included. So do you know who the woman comic in the leather pants is? Or are you just going to sit there and drink the booze I bought you and be as absolutely nasty as you can be?"

"Hmm. Are those my only two choices?"

Mary paused to think about it. "Actually, no there is a third choice. But I'm not sure you want to know what that is." Mary leaned in, let her coat open a little bit. Strong arming an old woman didn't rank real high on her list of personal achievements. But sometimes, the end justifies the means, no matter how distasteful it can get.

The old lady's tired and bleary eyes took in the gun, then came back up to Mary's face. "Tell you what," the old woman said. "One more of these and I'll tell you who she is. She's very attractive. You'd love to get her in the sack, I'm sure," she said.

"My prayers have been answered," Mary said and waved to the waitress. Moments later, another martini appeared in front of Ms. Venuta.

"Her name is Claudine. Claudine Greeling. It almost rhymes. She's cute, but not funny. Not funny at all. Her material is stuff Rita Rudner did ten, fifteen years ago. And did it better."

"Any idea where she might be tonight?"

"What, am I the goddamned Comedy Club Flyer?"

"You've been so helpful, Janet."

"Actually, I just saw her over at Schticky Fingers," the woman said. "The club on 14th and Wyoming. Don't know why I'm telling you. Maybe I just want you to get laid tonight. Improve your personality a little bit. Or maybe I'm hoping that you'll go away."

"I could only hope to be the kind, giving person you so clearly are," Mary said. "Does the Welcome Wagon know about you? Because you're giving them a run for their money."

"Welcome Wagon, that's good," the old lady said. "Maybe you should quit your job and go into comedy. Lord knows the world doesn't need another dumbass janitor. That's what you are, right?" The old woman leaned toward Mary and whispered, "Your clothes give it away, dear."

"Goodbye Janet," Mary said, getting up. "It's been a real pleasure."

"Don't forget to mop up before you leave!" the woman called out.

28

Schticky Fingers was sticky all over. Mary felt like she was part of a joke: Lady walks into a bar and says, hey, I'm looking for a woman in leather pants.

Luckily, Mary didn't have to ask anyone about Claudine Greeling. Mary spotted her right off. She was on stage. Her leather pants were gold, her shirt black. She had chestnut brown hair piled on top of her head. A pretty face and a knockout body. At least the fat heckler had good taste.

Mary got a beer and walked to the back of the seating area.

Despite the fair amount of people in the club and the haze of cigarette smoke, she spotted him right off.

A baseball cap, a big body stuffed into a small wooden chair. He had a bowl of chips in front of him and a bottle of beer. The suit looked odd on him, a black monstrosity that covered his enormous girth like a circus tent. And the baseball cap on top of his head seemed wildly out of place.

There was no point in approaching him now, Mary thought. He was probably in the middle of a fantasy starring himself and Claudine. No doubt involving the leather pants.

Mary found a table and sat down. This Claudine Greeling was going on about stupid boyfriends. Well, she could relate to that. She'd had more than her fair share. Like the guy who thought missile silos were actually disguised as real farm silos.

As Mary listened to Claudine's routine, she found herself chuckling. This woman was actually funny. That nasty talent agent didn't know what the hell she was talking about. That's probably why she was a talent scout stuck in these dives.

"Hey, I haven't seen you around here before." Mary turned to see a man in a striped shirt, green sport coat, and denim jeans. He had on black shoes, thick black glasses, and his dark hair was thick with gel. He was slightly cross-eyed.

"And you probably won't again," Mary said, taking a sip of her beer and not even looking at the guy.

"Jeez, tough room," he said.

"Not tough enough, apparently," Mary mumbled.

"I'm a comedian here," the guy said. He stuck out his hand. "Vince Killar. My friends call me Killer."

Mary ignored his hand. "Nice to meet you, Killer," she said. "My friends call me Gonnie."

"Gonnie? What is that, Italian?"

"No, it's a nickname. It's short for gonorrhea, which I've had for almost ten years. Really, really awful illness." Mary pushed out the chair next to her. "Want to sit with me for a while there Killer?"

"Um, I don't know....Gonnie."

The annoying guy had moved around in front of Mary and now she couldn't see the stage.

"I might take a rain check," he said. "But are you going to stay for my set? It's hot, I guarantee you that."

"Sounds lovely," Mary said. "But I actually have to go see

my urologist for a pressure wash. You know, the thing they use to clean patio decks?"

Mary leaned over to the side to get a look at the stage, but the comedian moved with her.

"Well tell your friends about me..." Killer said.

Mary abruptly stood up and saw that Claudine had left the stage and the big guy was gone, too.

"Shit," she said, then stood and pushed 'Killer' out of her way and hurried toward the stage. She immediately saw a short hallway to the office and dressing rooms, probably. There was also an exit door. She debated for just a moment. If the big guy had been following Miss Leather Pants around, he'd probably been barred from the dressing room. Mary hit the exit door and banged it open, then spilled out into an alley. The big guy was at the end, near a street.

"Hey!" she shouted.

The man turned, then immediately turned left and disappeared from view.

"Shit," Mary said. And then she started running. *If I can't catch this guy, I'm going to hang it up once and for all*, she thought.

29

The big man could move, Mary had to admit. Maybe he was in good shape from chasing down taco trucks. By the time she had gotten to the mouth of the alley and turned left, she barely caught sight of his freak ass baseball cap turning left on the next block up. Mary decided to turn left immediately and cut across the front lawn of an insurance company. She took a peek down an alley as she passed it, but she didn't see the big guy. However, she saw a pedestrian, an Asian woman with a Crate & Barrel shopping bag looking back over her shoulder as if she'd just seen the ghost of Shelley Winters skateboarding down the street.

By the time Mary hit the sidewalk and looked up toward the street ahead, Big Suit had hit the intersection and was turning right. He glanced over his shoulder and looked for her. Which was perfect, because by now she was right behind him and gaining.

He ran forward but Mary closed the gap quickly. Christ, I hope he doesn't have a cardiac before I get some information out of him, she thought.

Mary's breath started to come in gasps and she made a mental note to get back to her workouts.

Another block went by and she was within ten feet of him. He looked back over his shoulder and Mary saw his face, a pale mess covered with a thick sheen of sweat.

"Stop," she yelled. But he lowered his head and bulled his way ahead. Mary unleashed a burst of speed and jumped onto his back and rode him to the ground.

The .45 was in her hand and she put it in his face.

"Hey Mr. Happy Feet, how you doing?" she said.

The fat man gasped for air and now Mary really did worry that he would go into cardiac arrest. She felt his sweat seep into her shirt and a shiver ran down her back.

"Don't," he said.

"Oh, sure," she said. "Tell me what to do and I'll follow your every command. Just like you did when I told you to stop," Mary said through clenched teeth. This guy was a piece of work.

A couple walking down the sidewalk stopped at the sight of Mary holding a gun on the guy. The woman pulled a cell phone out of her purse. Mary didn't need the police right now.

"Pedophile," she said to them, nodding her head toward the big boy. "He would pretend to be a parade float to lure kids in. Trust me, he's gonna have a lot of boyfriends in prison."

The woman slid her cell phone back into her purse and the couple kept walking. Mary didn't even have to whip out her p.i. badge. Still, she would have to keep this quick.

"Get up, Slim," she said and pulled on the guy's big arm. He heaved to his feet and Mary pulled him up against the wall. To the right was a picture window of a little art studio.

A sculpture of a creature that seemed to be half dolphin and half woman looked down on them.

Mary stood slightly behind the big man, putting the .45 directly against his spine, just below his neck. To the casual passerby, it looked like she had her arm around him. A couple. Not the world's most attractive couple, but a couple nonetheless.

"Brent Cooper," Mary said. "Tell me what you know about his murder and I'll buy you a box of Twinkies. Tell me everything, right away, and I'll even throw in some Pop-Tarts."

"I don't know what you're talking about." Still heaving from the exertion, the big boy's voice was high and girlish. Mary knew it would be.

Mary pressed the muzzle of the .45 harder against his spine, although she couldn't actually find any vertebrae beneath the Serta mattress-type padding. But she did the best she could do.

"Nice try, Bones," she said. "Are you a struggling actor? You do method, don't you?"

"What?"

"Let me see your SAG card. Or don't you have one yet? Because I have to tell you, that lie about not knowing anything, you didn't pull it off very well. Do you need me to give you your motivation?"

The man breathed in ragged gasps as an answer.

"Listen Hambone," Mary said. "Tell me what you know about Brent Cooper's murder or you won't make it to that big cardiac arrest you're heading toward."

"I don't know who the hell you're talking about."

"The guy who got murdered behind the Leg Pull? The guy who ripped you to shreds in front of a whole bunch of people who can easily identify you? Ring any bells?"

The big man sighed, his breath had slowed and he mopped his face with a forearm. The dark material of his suit came away slick with sweat. "Oh, that. Well, we had some words and I left. That's it. End of story."

"You left? You didn't wait for him outside? You didn't cut him open because he'd ripped you to shreds?"

"No! I don't like violence. I don't fight. I run. Or try to."

"But you're fighting me now. Lying to me."

"Listen, I didn't do anything."

"That's not what people are saying at the Leg Pull. They're saying you two had words and that..."

"Who's saying that?"

"Everyone."

He suddenly looked worried and Mary saw an opening so she went full bore right through it.

"They've told *me*. But they haven't told the cops."

"You're not a cop?"

"You're so perceptive. I love that."

"What are you?"

"A concerned family member. And a strong believer in revenge. The cops are the least of your worries. I may just leave your brains all over Ocean Avenue. Sound good?"

His eyes flashed wildly around, panic behind them.

"Look at it this way, you can either tell me," she said. "Or you've had your last In-N-Out burger."

He let out a long breath that smelled like onion rings. It doesn't matter how big they are, Mary thought. They all break, eventually.

"This guy said he was a friend of Brent Cooper's," the man said. "I'd never heard of this Cooper guy. I was there to see Claudine - did you see her? She's great..." His eyes got all dreamy and Mary could see the beginning of another fantasy come into his brain.

"Focus, Pudge. Focus."

"Anyway. This guy slipped me a fifty and said to heckle this Brent Cooper guy. So I did. That Cooper guy was an asshole. He just went crazy saying all kinds of nasty shit."

"What did the guy look like? The guy who told you to do this?"

"He was an old guy, I don't know. You've been in the club, it's dark."

"We'll come back to that. So he told you to heckle Brent, then what?"

"Then I was supposed to act like I wanted to fight him and sort of nod toward the alley."

"Did you?"

"Yeah. But I didn't go out there! I got scared and took off."

"Smart move."

"Look, I had nothing to do with all that. It was supposed to be a joke, I didn't know the guy was going to get killed."

"Let's go back to the old guy."

"Oh my God," he said.

Mary felt him jerk. "What?"

"There he is." Mary began to look across the street where the guy's eyes were looking, but she never finished her scan.

The fat man's head snapped back against the brick wall and Mary felt a gush of warmth on her hand. Blood and brain matter poured from the back of his head. He slumped against her as another bullet hit him in the chest. Shards of brick bit into Mary's neck as a bullet exploded next to her ear. She tried to push against the fat man but as his body sagged to the sidewalk, it took her with it. She found herself trapped beneath him, struggling to get free.

She looked over his shoulder across the street. An old

man in a turquoise blue windbreaker stood just behind a tree, his gun blocked from view. She saw him step to the right, saw the gun with the attached silencer.

Mary held her arm up and over the big man, then fired a quick shot at the old guy across the street.

Mary got one leg beneath her and pushed upward, heaved with all of her strength, and rolled the huge man over. She was able to squirm out from underneath him.

Across the street, the old man's gun spat again and glass from the art studio's window showered down upon her. She had no choice. She got to her feet, crouched, and then dove over the art studio's display shelf into the showroom itself. The dolphin woman sculpture exploded and pieces of metal, paper mache, and wire rained down on Mary's back. The head and shoulders of the sculpture were still intact, so she took cover behind them and fired at the old man. She steadied her hand and reeled off shot after shot, emptying her entire clip in a matter of seconds.

Mary's ears rang and the smell of gunpowder assaulted her senses. She ducked back down and thumbed the magazine release, grabbed her spare from her coat pocket, slammed it in, then wiped her bloody hand off on a piece of curtain that had been shot off the window.

Bullets exploded around her.

Mary waited out the last of the explosions then rolled and popped up just over the display platform. The blue windbreaker caught her eye. He'd moved two trees over and was slapping another clip into his gun.

She let out a breath, and waited for him to step away from the tree.

He did.

Mary fired twice fast. The double tap.

The man went down in a heap.

Mary vaulted over the display platform and onto the sidewalk, nearly slipping on the concrete's coating of glass and blood. She raced across the street, her gun held out in front of her just in case the old shooter was playing possum.

But once she got to him, stood over him and looked at the blood gushing from his mouth, she knew it was no act.

"Who *are* you?" she said.

A weird sucking sound came from his chest and his mouth opened.

"Aaauegh," he said and then his eyes went still. Pink bubbles came out of his nose.

"Huh, is that an Arabic name?" Mary said.

Sirens sounded in the distance.

Mary reached into his coat pocket, nothing but more clips. Her hands shook slightly and her legs felt weak. Her breath was shallow and for a moment she thought she would faint.

Mary searched him and found a slim wallet in his pocket. She flipped it open to his California driver's license.

Noah Baxter.

She'd never heard of him.

30

L APD's finest arrived and Mary surrendered her weapon and submitted to a search. They put her in the back of a squad car while the patrol cops wandered around, waiting for the detectives and crime scene technicians to show up.

Mary sniffed. The car smelled vaguely of vomit. Maybe it was the cop's cologne. Eau de regurgitation.

Probably some drunk on his way to the tank had tossed his Chips Ahoys back here. The patrol cops were in charge of cleaning their own vehicles if something like that happened, Mary knew. This had obviously been cleaned by a man. Most guys she knew, the only way they could clean something was with a Swiffer.

Out of the corner of her eye she saw the flash of some fish-belly white skin. Mary turned just as Jake and the Shark got out of their detective's car.

"Fun has officially arrived," Mary said under her breath. She looked at the Shark and the way she assumed instant command of the scene. But God she was pale. The ME guys might mistake her for the corpse.

Mary shivered. It wasn't the first time she had killed someone. But it wasn't easy. She forced it from her mind, but suddenly a chill would shoot down her spine and her stomach would do flip flops.

A couple of the uniforms were talking to the pair of detectives, gesturing and pointing with their hands and occasionally looking over at the patrol car.

"Yeah, hi," Mary said, watching the Shark. "Go to hell, uh-huh, hello," she said. Mary felt off-kilter. She'd just shot and killed an old man, for God's sake. The adrenaline had worn off and now she just felt tired and cranky. She pictured her bed back in her apartment. She wanted to curl up inside the warm blankets and not come out for a few months.

Mary saw the tall, pale woman nod toward the car and immediately one of the patrol cops turned and walked toward her. Jake shot her a look as if to say, "There's nothing I can do right now."

"Yeah, yeah," Mary said under her breath again, just as the patrol cop opened up the driver's door and got behind the wheel.

"Did someone puke in here or is your gym bag in the trunk?" Mary said.

The cop put the car in gear and ignored her. They drove away from the scene and Mary instantly felt a touch better.

"I mean, jeez, it smells like a French whore with a purse full of gorgonzola," she said.

The cop looked over his shoulder at her. "I'm taking you downtown," he said.

"Downtown? Oh, that's lovely. We can do some shopping...go get a pedicure--"

"Ma'am, I hope you realize how serious this is."

When they pulled up at a stoplight, he looked up at the rearview mirror. Mary saw that he was a young guy. Probably the lowest ranking of anyone at the scene. He looked a little green around the gills. Maybe he'd never seen a dead person before. He'd probably looked at both the big guy and the old man. Neither one of them looked very good.

Mary had seen more than her fair share. She should probably be more sensitive to the poor kid.

"Serious," Mary said. "Yes. Very serious. So how do you like Sergeant Davies? Did you know she's made out of wax?"

The young cop ignored her and guided the patrol car smoothly onto the I-10 freeway.

"Never mind," Mary said, once they'd settled into a lane. "Sergeant Davies. What do you think of her?

"How do you know her?" he finally said.

"Hey, just answer the question."

He looked at her in the rearview mirror. Couldn't decide whether to be offended at her tone, or to answer. He chose to answer.

"She's...good," he said.

"That's what I call a ringing endorsement."

"Well, I mean. You know, smart. Efficient."

"Now you're gushing."

"She—"

"Do you think she's hot?"

"Ma'am, I'd rather not...I'm driving. And you're involved in a double homicide. I don't think I should be talking to you about our detectives."

Mary nodded to him in the rearview mirror.

"Is she still messing around with that Cornell guy?"

"Okay," the young cop said. "That's it. I'm going to stop talking now."

"Just tell me the office scuttlebutt. Are they still a couple?"

He looked in the mirror again at her, as he took the exit for downtown proper.

"That's the rumor," he said.

Mary laid her head back on the seat and watched L.A. fly past her window.

You never knew with rumors. Jake had said it was a one-night stand. Well, if it was more than that, good for Jake. Might help him get promoted faster. They made a nice couple.

Kind of like Satan and Judas.

31

The cop allowed her to go to the bathroom, then brought her a cup of coffee in an actual coffee cup. The cup read "Death Valley National Park." Nice.

"How appropriate," Mary said. She took a sip. It was awful.

They left her alone for an hour. Goddamn Jake. How could he leave her in here this long, knowing she'd just killed someone? The depths of his treachery were deepening every day. He was probably picking up the Shark's dry cleaning, trying to improve the scores on his performance review at the end of the year.

Or else they were just killing time to make her more willing to talk. Bastards.

After another fifteen minutes of waiting, the door opened and Jake walked in. He looked tired and frazzled. Mary had no sympathy for him.

"All done debriefing your boss?" Mary said.

Jake stopped. "What's that supposed to mean?"

Mary put a finger to her chin. "Hmm. What could that mean? What could the subtext possibly be?"

He let out a heavy sigh and dropped a file folder on the desk. "This isn't the time," Jake said.

"That's what you said last time," Mary said. "She's really got you under control – did she put a dog collar on you and call you dirty names-"

"Mary," he said through gritted teeth. "You're not doing yourself any good." Jake's eyes snaked over toward the mirror.

"I know she's listening," Mary said. "Probably watching your tough guy interrogation tactics and touching herself every time you-"

"Cut the shit and tell me what happened."

Mary raised an eyebrow at his flaring temper.

"Oooh," she said. "I think you just made her moan."

Jake ground his jaws together. "What. Happened."

Mary sighed. "Okay. I actually do have a confession to make. Are you sure I shouldn't have my lawyer here?"

"Come on, Mary," he said, his voice softer and his body relaxing. "It's me."

"Okay," Mary said, nodding as if she'd reached a decision. "My confession. Here it is."

She let the pause hang for a moment.

"I'm a chubby chaser. I like tubby guys."

Jake's eyes went half-mast.

"That big guy I was with?" she said. "I planned to take his giant ass home and screw his brains out. There's nothing I like more than grabbing a couple handfuls of Dubuque ham-"

The door banged open and the Shark walked in.

"Jake, I'll take over."

"Ooh," Mary said. "I think you've just been demoted Jake."

"Shut up," Davies said.

Mary rolled her eyes. "Potty mouth," she said.

"Jake," the Shark said. "Out."

Jake turned and headed for the door.

"I bet he likes it when you boss him around, doesn't he?" Mary said. "I can tell you're the Alpha Male in the relationship, that's for sure. Does he have food bowls with his name on them?"

The door slammed shut and the sound reverberated in the small room. Davies said nothing. She just looked at Mary, gathering herself. Mary looked back at her. One eyebrow raised.

"What's the problem?" Mary said. "I really do like the plus-sized guys."

The Shark nodded. "How about we help each other out?" she said.

"You mean...cooperate?"

"You give us some information, we'll give you some information."

"That sounds very Democratic," Mary said. "Very American."

"So tell me something. Anything."

Mary nodded. "That makes sense. Perfect sense. Okay, here's what I know-"

The door burst open and slammed against the opposite wall.

"That's enough!" Whitney Braggs said as he walked into the room accompanied by a tall, regal woman with a pinched face and frizzy hair.

"I'm Joan Hessburg," the woman said. She handed a card to Davies. "I am an attorney and Mary Cooper is my client," the woman said. "Are you charging her with a crime, Detective?"

The Shark looked like a pile of horse manure had just been dropped at her feet.

"The cavalry led by Bob Barker," Mary said. "I love it!"

"Sons of bitches kept us waiting for a half hour," Braggs said and glared at Davies.

Mary shook her head. The guy looked like a walking advertisement for Nautica but beat people up and had the mouth of a Navy construction worker.

"Let's go, Miss Cooper," her new attorney said. She gave the Shark her card. "Contact me if you wish to further question my client."

The Shark took the card and threw it on the floor, then headed for the door.

Mary turned to Braggs and her new attorney.

"You got here just in time," Mary said. She nodded toward the departing Davies. "She was going to do a full cavity search on me. But here's the awful part, she said she was going to have me do one on her afterward."

Mary shook her head, and looked toward the mirror. "Sicko."

32

M ary needed a drink, and she invited Braggs and the attorney. Of course, Ms. Hessburg begged off. Time is money was the unspoken excuse. She left Mary with a card and a lingering scent of Chanel. Or maybe J. Lo.

Mary had killed before. She'd shot an insane husband set on killing his ex-wife. She'd killed a drug dealer determined to kill her client's son for some sort of supposed deal gone bad.

Each time, there was a delayed reaction. Initially, the justification was enough. Over time, however, it wasn't easy. It was like a darkish cloud hanging over her for awhile. The immediate solution? Booze.

But Mary had to clean herself. So she had Braggs drive her home and sent him out for drinks. If the guy was going to be around, he might as well be useful. By the time she had showered, Braggs showed up with enough bottles of beer, booze, and wine to satisfy a fraternity during Rush week.

She requested a double Jack Daniels on the rocks.

Braggs quickly complied. Mary sat on the couch. She didn't want to look out at the water, but she did.

"Have you ever had a lychee martini?" Braggs asked.

"If you live in L.A., you have to," Mary said.

She heard him using a shaker and turned to see him pouring its contents into a martini glass. He came over and sat to her left, in a club chair facing the ocean.

"Do you want to talk about it?" he asked. The smooth voice had taken on the role of trusted confidante.

"No."

"Okay."

"Do you know who Noah Baxter is?" she said.

"Of course," he said, and took a sip of his martini. Mary looked down at her drink. A bunch of ice. She held it out and shook it at Braggs. He hopped up and refreshed it, then brought it back to her.

"So?" she said.

"We all knew him," Braggs said. "He was a stand-up, just like all of us. But he was the worst of the worst. He had a really, really dark sense of humor that never came across well with audiences. He shocked them instead of making them laugh. Not a good trait for a comedian."

He drank from his martini and Mary drained half of her Jack on the rocks.

"He ended up writing for other comedians, who would take his stuff and lighten it up a little bit. It really wasn't that bad, it just needed a little bit of...sanity."

"Yeah, that's the impression I had of him," Mary said. Already her brain was going slightly numb. It felt good.

"But eventually, his stuff fell out of favor and as I recall, he had some personal problems. Drinking, drugs, or something." Braggs waved his hand around as if a mosquito were bothering him.

"And then?" Mary said.

"And then he bought a one-way ticket to the Land of Hollywood Forgottens. It's a community that keeps growing, every day. Easy to get into, very difficult to get out."

Mary nodded. Of course. He went where it seemed like every lead in the case of her uncle's murder had gone: nowhere.

Her glass looked empty so she held it out to Braggs again. He refilled hers and his own, then came back.

"I thought I heard some rumors about him getting a job in Las Vegas or something," Braggs said. "Managing some female comedian, but that was it. He fell off of everyone's radar."

Mary nodded. Her head felt like it had put on ten pounds.

"There's a million guys like Noah Baxter," Braggs said. "A little flash of success, then a disappearing act when they realize the big payday is never going to come. Most of them don't even realize it's over. Can't admit it to themselves. It's really kind of sad. Of course, I can't speak from experience. It's just that I'm very sympathetic-"

Mary stretched out and put her head on a pillow. She drank awkwardly from her glass, but she got the Jack down. Drinking Jack made her think of Jake. Jake the Jerk. She giggled.

"I might know someone who could tell us more about Noah," Braggs said.

"Oh, yeah?" Mary said. Her voice was thick with sleepiness.

"Margaret Stewart."

"Martha Stewart? The domestic goddess?"

"No, *Margaret* Stewart," Braggs said.

"Who the hell is that?" Mary slurred.

"She used to be my agent. And Brent's agent. And Noah's agent."

"Lady gets around."

"In fact, she was everybody's agent back then. A powerhouse."

Mary closed her eyes and the first faint stirrings of sleep, like the start of the incoming tide, slowly swept across her forehead.

"I think I'm going to fall asleep," she said, a sound suspiciously similar to snoring began to come from her mouth. "You can let yourself out-" she started to say, but never finished the sentence.

"She knew everyone," Braggs said. "But most of all, she knew where all the skeletons were. That's more valuable than anything for sale on Rodeo Drive, that's for sure."

Mary fell asleep then, an image of the old man she'd shot as a skeleton, dancing around in the dark.

er eyes grated open, like stone doors in an Egyptian tomb. Mary stared at the ceiling for several minutes, rewinding the film of last night, watching it in reverse order. She didn't like what she saw.

Mary pushed back the blankets and sat up. Her head hurt and her stomach ached. She walked out to the kitchen and made coffee, then stood with her head hanging down while it brewed. Extra cream and extra sugar went in to bolster her recovery. She sat at the kitchen table and a little yellow note caught her attention.

10 a.m. Margaret Stewart.

It was signed Whitney Braggs. And there was an address scribbled next to Margaret Stewart's name. Mary looked at the clock.

She had forty-five minutes to shower, dress, and get out to Beverly Hills.

Great.

Mary started for the shower and slipped off her robe, then froze.

She had on her pink pajamas. She thought for a

moment, and then a horrifying thought nearly drove her to her knees.

Had she put them on herself?

Or had Braggs?

Suddenly, her head hurt even worse.

34

M argaret Stewart's face was so taut from plastic surgery that Mary worried it would snap and fly across the office like a Frisbee. She had the urge to go over and plunk out a rhythm on it like a tribal drum. Didn't the woman have a constant headache?

"That was quite a group," Ms. Stewart said. Mary guessed the woman's age to be seventy-ish, and thought the voice matched the skin: tight and unforgiving. Mary glanced around the office. Black leather, polished chrome, black-and-white photography. Typical power agent office.

"Yes, dysfunction in large numbers." Mary said. "Always the hallmark of a good time."

They'd already done the necessary introductions and had started in on the history of Brent Cooper and his gang.

"They certainly took the party with them," Ms. Stewart said. "And it was always a *big* party."

"In what way? Drugs? Gambling? Monkeys in lingerie?" Mary asked.

"Lingerie, yes. Monkeys no. At least, no monkeys at the

parties I went to. I'm sure at some point, animals were involved."

"Anything criminal going on?" Mary said. "Anything that would make someone come back later and start killing people?"

Margaret Stewart shrugged her shoulders, then nodded at Braggs. "Why don't you ask him? He was there."

Braggs shook his head. "Not like you," he said. "I had gigs, flew around, didn't see those guys and gals for months at a time. You were there constantly."

"Besides," Mary chimed in. "You probably knew everyone. And you most likely knew them better than he did. Braggs here, from what he tells me, just hung out and partied. He was probably busy de-flowering the female population of Beverly Hills."

"It would be arrogant of me to agree with you, but I must confess that's a fairly accurate statement," Braggs said.

"I'm thinking they confided more in you," Mary said to Ms. Stewart. "You know, crying to the agent about all of their problems and issues. That's the stuff we need to know about."

"That's very perceptive, Ms. Cooper," Margaret said. "But I was their agent not their babysitter and I did not perform confessions. They didn't tell me everything because if they had problems, they certainly didn't want anyone to know about them, especially their agent."

"Yes, I'm sure all actors and actresses prevent their agent from witnessing their neuroses firsthand," Mary said. "Come on, Margaret. This is L.A. Agents know where all the bodies are buried. Or at least who put the bodies where. And they're good bodies because it's L.A. and everyone works out."

"Here's what I meant," Margaret Stewart said. "I just said

they didn't come and blab all of their war stories to me. Yeah, I heard some stories. Some were true, most of them were probably not."

"Why don't you tell us about the ones that were probably true? If there actually were any."

The older woman pushed back from her desk and crossed her legs. She let out a long breath.

"That was a long time ago," she said. "Let's see. There was a core group. Brent Cooper was definitely one of the ringleaders. God he was a smartass. Arrogant, pushy, and a vicious mouth. You remind me of him," she said to Mary.

"That's one compliment I never get tired of hearing," Mary said.

"Let's see, there was also Harvey Mitchell," Margaret said. "He was a star even back then. God, I had to turn away so much work for him. Even modeling agencies wanted a piece of him."

"Harvey Mitchell?" Mary asked. "The host of The Night Talker?"

"The one and only," Braggs said.

The Night Talker was a long-standing hit for NBC. Not quite the Tonight Show, but still a very powerful ratings earner. Harvey Mitchell was the silver-haired host. Interviewing stars, doing skits, and having a great time doing it. Making boodles of cash, too.

"There were so many of them," Margaret Stewart said. "They floated in and out. Look, why don't I just do this? When Mr. Braggs called me, I went into my archives and pulled my files for everyone I could think of. Including Noah Baxter's. Obviously, there's no longer anything sensitive in them. Half of the people are dead or disappeared."

She gestured at a chair near a filing cabinet. There was a box full of faded yellow folders, thick with papers inside.

"Like I mentioned before," Margaret said. "People came, people went. Men, women, kids, animals. Everything that could have possibly gone on among prosperous entertainment people in Los Angeles during those days definitely went on." The woman glanced at her phone then continued. "So you can guess most of what was occurring on a daily, and nightly, basis. Why don't you just look through all that, and then if you have any questions, call me. It's not like I have time to sit here and tell you about every last thing, plus, at my age, I'd probably get most of it wrong. So just take the stuff, look it over and call me if you have any more questions. Okay?"

Braggs walked over and picked up the box.

Mary stood. "Thank you Ms. Stewart. I'm sure you'll be happy to know that I most likely am going to call you again. I always have questions to ask. It's one of my character traits that makes me irresistible to both sexes."

"Brent Cooper. Reincarnated," the older woman said and turned back to her computer as if they'd already left.

"Ouch," Mary said on her way out.

35

M ary ditched Braggs as soon as possible.

"Don't you want to go through that stuff together?" he'd asked, looking at the files.

"I think we've gone through enough together, don't you?" Mary said.

"Not really," he said. "But everyone's certainly entitled to their opinion, no matter how wrong that opinion may be."

"Before I go," he said. "The rest of your clients are here. You remember the consortium of Brent's old gang that together sent me to hire you?"

"Well, they're all here and would like to get together with you. You know, go over the case and how they can help you catch the killer. I know it's short notice, but does tonight work?"

"I've always got time for senior citizens," Mary said. It would be a good chance for her to dig for more information anyway.

"Don't look so excited, Mary. They're actually a fun bunch."

"Laugh a minute, I'm sure, Whitney."

Braggs smiled, his white teeth gleaming in the late Hollywood sun.

"I understand," he said. "I'm cramping your style. Too much too soon, I take it?"

"That would presuppose I have a style, Braggs."

"Oh you've got style. Plenty of it."

"Are you hitting on me?"

"Absolutely not," he said, holding his hands wide, a gesture of pure innocence. "That would be scandalous. A man my age making improper advances on a deceased colleague's lovely, sexy niece? One who is clearly entertaining the idea of benefiting from an older man's hard-earned experience in the bedroom? No."

"The only thing I'm experiencing right now is revulsion mixed with a small amount of nausea."

"Understood, Mary. Understood. However, I'm not hitting on you, despite the wonderful curve of your–"

"I am armed, Braggs."

Braggs snapped his mouth shut, a mischievous twinkle in his eye.

Mary walked away, wondering if some old ladies somewhere were supplying Braggs with Viagra. If not, she should set him up with the Golden Girls at Brent's place. They'd tear him apart.

36

Margaret Stewart hadn't been lying. At least not about the files. They were old. As old as the Hollywood Hills that had spawned the careers of these actors, comedians, and writers. She set the stack of files down on her desk next to her computer and fired up the machine.

Mary clicked on the iPod that ran her office sound system, and chose an album by Brandi Carlile, an immensely talented singer songwriter from Seattle who Mary had seen in concert. An incredible voice.

She launched her Internet browser, then followed that with her People Search software. It was a proprietary program developed by a friend of Mary's, a software developer at a large corporation who had been fired for trying to improve the company's product. It's never a wise move to be so good in corporate America that you threaten your boss's livelihood. Mary had helped out on his case and in return he had pirated software, improved it, and given it to her as a gift.

Now, Mary began alphabetizing the files. After fifteen minutes, she had all seventy-five files in order by last name.

With that, she launched into the job at hand. Namely, using her software to find, locate, and hopefully eliminate as many people as she could from the pile. The good thing was, one of the forms required by Margaret Stewart had included a section for personal information, and a line for the client's social security number. That eliminated any problems with two Michael Williamses.

The pictures, the head shots, made Mary pause. God, they had all looked so young and happy. And real. She smiled at the credits. Television shows that she'd never heard of. Comedy reviews, clubs and movies she'd never heard of. It had been a different world back then.

The first conclusion Mary reached was that Uncle Brent's crew didn't have great longevity. Of the first ten files, seven were dead. Not surprising, though. Depending on how old they were when they made the L.A. attempt, and what year they launched, the majority of the folks were somewhere between sixty and eighty. Despite L.A.'s current reputation for health conscious individuals, back then they all smoked and drank like fish. Cancer had gotten lots of them, most likely.

She then dove into the files, working as quickly as possible. It took her just under two hours to eliminate everyone she could. By the time she was done, she was left with a very manageable keeper pile. Twenty-six living, five unaccounted for. After all the illnesses, the car wrecks, the suicides, these twenty-six had made it through. She silently congratulated them. The five who were unaccounted for, well, she would make up her mind about them later.

The twenty-six living would be relatively simple. She would have to track them down, interview them if possible, and cross them off the list until theoretically, she got the pool down to a chosen few and then she would have to take it from there.

It was the five unaccounted for that would be the bigger challenge. They had completely fallen off the grid, as the law enforcement community liked to call it. Or, just as likely, had taken themselves off the grid. Running from the law. Running from loan sharks. Hiding from ex-wives and alimony payments. She already pictured a couple of the guys bagging groceries in Florida under assumed names.

More people abandoned their identities than most realized. The process really wasn't that difficult. The fact that most people thought it was difficult was why more didn't do it.

There was a definite appeal to tossing out your current station in life, and starting an entirely new one.

She couldn't blame them if that's what they'd done.

At some point, hadn't everyone fantasized about disappearing and starting over somewhere new? Just wiping the slate clean? The ultimate do-over?

Mary couldn't speak for everyone.

But she knew she'd considered it.

37

M ary drove back to her place and was at her door when she heard him.

"Hey, hold up!"

She turned and saw the new good-looking neighbor trot down the hall toward her. What was his name again, she thought? Chris. Chris McAllister.

"Sorry," he said when he finally reached her. "But I wanted to ask you a question." He hesitated. "Actually, I'd like to get your opinion."

"Yes, I think global warming is actually happening. Soon we'll be underwater. Might be an improvement for L.A."

He laughed, displaying that easy confidence she had noticed and liked, before.

"You know, I happen to agree, but I actually wanted your opinion on something else?"

"Hey, you want 'em, opinions I got."

"It's actually my apartment. I can't decide where to hang two paintings. I needed a different perspective."

"Ah, so when you bring your lady friends here they'll feel at home? Sort of some inside information?"

"Exactly. I want you to spy on your gender for me. Come back and tell me *everything*."

Mary chuckled and then her mind flashed back to the shooting at the gallery where the mermaid/dolphin had been destroyed.

"You know," she said. "Art and I don't have a great history together."

"Oh, come on," he said. "It'll only take a minute."

"All right, I'll tell my manservant Jacques to keep the lobster warm."

He laughed, and for a brief moment Mary realized it was a laugh she could get used to.

Chris McAllister opened the door and Mary followed him in, checking out his ass as she went. Nice. It was firm and taut. She wanted to bounce a quarter off the damn thing, or maybe something else. Something more personal.

"Sorry for the mess," he said.

Mary looked around. Mess? Her place hadn't been this neat and clean since she'd moved in.

"Yeah, what a dump," she said. "Sheesh. If you think this is bad, come over and make a mess of my place. It'll be a huge improvement."

It was a nice place. He'd bought completely contemporary furnishings. Sleek tables. Fifties style lamps. But not over the top. Not self-conscious. She had to admit, it was just good taste. Hip good taste.

"Before I present the dilemma," he said. "Can I offer the judge a beverage? Wine? Martini? Beer?"

"Do you have any grain alcohol?" she said. "200 proof?"

"Sorry," he said. "Just polished that off last night."

"In that case, I'm good for now." Her head still ached from the Jack Daniels. She was looking forward to going to bed.

"Okay, here's the deal," he said. "As you can see, my overall style is eclectic, but I've got two pieces of art here."

He led her to the living room where two large canvases sat. One was definitely in the impressionistic camp. Heavy brushstrokes.

The other was like a Giclee print. It was an electric guitar.

"Hmm," Mary said.

"What?"

"Well, I like both," she said.

"Oh come on," Chris answered. "My impression of you was that you don't pull any punches. What do I look like? A pansy? I can handle the truth." He raised his eyebrows and did a reasonably good impression of Jack Nicholson from A Few Good Men. "You need me on that wall..."

"Does anyone actually use the word pansy anymore?" Mary said.

"Only pansies."

They both laughed.

"Okay, I'll be honest," Mary said. "Which is something I haven't been in a long time. In fact, the last time I was honest I actually strained an abdominal muscle."

"Okay."

"The guitar print fits better, but the impressionistic painting is a better piece of art. It's really good. Even though it doesn't fit, wouldn't you want to go with the better art?"

She turned to look at her neighbor. He wasn't even looking at the art. He was looking at her.

"I agree with you," he said. "The funny thing is, that one-" he said, pointing to the guitar painting. "That one cost me a ton. And that one," he said, pointing to the impression-istic piece. "That one I got for twenty bucks at an estate sale."

"I didn't figure you for a bargain hunter."

"Oh, yeah?" he said. "What *did* you figure me for?"

"I figured you for some sort of circus performer."

"Good guess. But I'm actually a chef."

"Wow, what a coincidence. I love to have other people cook for me."

Chris checked his watch. "Speaking of food, I was just going to whip up some pasta. Wanna stay?"

He turned and headed for the kitchen.

Mary checked out his ass again.

"I suppose I could cancel my dinner with the Governor."

38

Mary woke up in her own apartment. But only because she had insisted that she do so. The night had been wonderful. Good food. Great conversation and so much more.

She poured herself a cup of coffee and looked at the stack of files in front of her. But her mind went back to Chris McAllister. Mary had never slept with anyone that soon – it was only the second time she'd talked with him. A part of her felt guilty and ashamed. A part of her told her she was middle-aged and that those kind of rules no longer applied.

She felt a small shudder when she considered that she could end up like those three nymphomaniacs who had supplied Uncle Brent with his Viagra.

Mary shelved her thoughts of carnal pleasures and called Braggs. She got his voicemail.

"Braggs, it's Mary Cooper," she said. "Change your message, you sound like one of those god-awful announcers for the tractor pull." She growled her voice. "Sunday! Sunday! Sunday! Get ready for the Monster Truck Rally-"

"Whitney Braggs here," he said, cutting her off.

"Put down the Brylcreem and meet me at Alice's. You can finish your French pedicure later."

"It seems you think I'm a bit of a dandy."

"Perish the thought, Princess. Just meet me there in ten minutes."

"Affirmative."

"Shut up, Braggs."

Silence.

"Tell your old cronies to dust off the mothballs and meet us there, too."

"Ah yes," he said. "The 'old gang' as it were. I'll get them there as absolutely soon as possible."

"And tell them if they have any old pictures, mementos, letters, to bring them, too. Ixnay on anything pornographic."

"They're not those kind of men, Mary."

"I was talking about you."

39

They filed in like a parade of Hollywood glamour gone bad. Faces too tan. Or too pale. Bodies too thin. Or too flabby. Teeth too white. Or too yellow. If there were teeth at all.

Braggs introduced each new arrival to Mary, and gave her a brief rundown of their background. Mary recognized most of them from Margaret Stewart's files. She noted each one as they were introduced, adding their faces to her mental Rolodex.

Jason Prescott. Really tall. 6'6" easy. Former stand-up comic turned MC of old folks comedy shows.

Mark Reihm. Average looking except for the severe acne scarring on his face. A gray buzz cut heightened the disastrous effect.

Franklin Goslyn. A little bowling ball of a man.

Todd Castro. A white-haired, dark-skinned guy light on personality, heavy on horrible cologne. Most likely purchased at Marshalls, TJMaxx, or Ross Superstores.

Eventually, the names, faces and handshakes, and hugs

bordering on ass grabs were over and Mary got down to business.

"All right," she said to the assembled group. "We've got work to do, fellas. You guys can jerk each other off later."

The group slowly quieted down.

"Nice hooters!" a voice shouted out. Chuckles and guffaws filled the air.

"Save it for your Inflate-A-Mate." Mary said.

More laughter followed Mary's comment.

"Now that's what I call 'junk in the trunk'!" one of the old men said.

"Baby got back, front, top, and bottom!" another guy said.

"That's some quality material guys," Mary said. "I can't believe no one else noticed your talents."

Braggs, sitting in the front, turned back and gave the stinkeye to the rabble rousers. They quieted down and Mary used the opportunity to lay out the files of the five people she had failed to identify.

"Look, she's spreading herself out," a voice said.

"Right on the table?"

"Giddyup!" Someone added the sound of horse hooves. Clip clop, clip clop.

Mary picked up the first file, ignoring the barely concealed laughter.

"Martin Gulinski," she said, and held up the first file.

"Farty Marty!"

"He's been dead for ten years, and while he was alive, he smelled like he'd died ten years ago!"

Mary took out a pen and sighed.

"As much as I enjoy the colorful commentary," she said. "Let's try to stick to dead or alive, current whereabouts, next of kin."

"He changed his name," this from a guy sitting in the middle of the group. He sort of looked like Mickey Rooney. "Gulinski was too ethnic. He thought he wasn't getting work because of it. So he changed it to Gulls and then got cancer and died. Should've stuck with Gulinski."

"He had children," another man added. "I think in Portland. He could never figure out why they were black kids. Looked just like the UPS man."

Mary rolled her eyes. "The kids. Boys or girls?"

"Two boys, I think."

Mary wrote down "Gulinski," and "Portland." She'd look the sons up and call them, try to confirm that their father was indeed dead. She'd leave the flatulence part out.

Next file.

"Marie Stevens," she said.

"Dead!"

"She's not dead. She just disappeared."

"OD'd in the seventies." This was from Braggs.

"She was always a partier," another guy added. "I think I tapped that."

"You couldn't tap a quarter barrel, Roger."

"Children?" Mary said.

"Thank God no. The Devil's Spawn. She was crazy."

"Where was she from?"

"Wisconsin."

"Texas."

"She wasn't from anywhere else. She was from here. A native."

"No way! Marie was crazy! You couldn't believe a word she said."

"Family?" Mary asked.

"No way," a man said. "She was too 'out there.' I think

she probably didn't have family – that's why there's nothing on her."

"Pauper's grave, probably."

"You know what they call dead bodies in L.A.?" a guy in the back called out.

"What?"

"Studio audiences!"

Mary tried to keep her patience.

"Jesus Christ, you guys don't know anything," a guy standing near the doorway to Alice's kitchen said. "Marie's buried at Forest Hills, for fuck's sake. Harvey Mitchell paid for the whole thing. The burial and stuff."

"Where is that bastard anyway?" someone said. "Is he at the proctologist again or is he just too good for us?"

"The procto's – he goes every day!"

Mary wrote down 'Forest Hills' next to Marie Stevens' information.

She pulled out the next file.

"Matthew Bolt."

"Fatty Matty!"

"He's in the union. An electrician or something."

"That fuck couldn't change a light bulb!"

"Hey, how many proctologists does it take to change a light bulb?"

Silence.

"As soon as he takes his finger out of my ass I'll ask him!"

Again with the proctologist gag, Mary thought. No wonder these guys were bagging groceries at the Albertson's.

Mary wrote down "Union electrician" next to Matt Bolt's name.

The next file.

"Betty Miller."

"Ready Betty!"

Too bad nicknames weren't a lucrative industry, Mary thought. These guys would have been rich.

"Man she was great," said the Castro guy. With all the cologne. "You could always count on Betty for a good screw. At one party she did like six or seven guys."

"Yeah, in six or seven minutes."

"Speak for yourself, Speed Shot," Castro snapped back.

"She moved back to New York," someone added. "Got married. Did some plays. Bulked up and died of a heart attack, I think."

"Anyone know her married name?" Mary said.

"She married a poor Jew. Didn't know there were any in New York."

"Guy's name was Schneider."

"If you find her," one old man advised Mary. "Lift her up and check underneath – he might be squished."

Mary wrote down "New York" and Betty Schneider, left out the squished bit.

"Last one," Mary said, and picked up the remaining file. "David Kenum."

There was silence.

"No cool nicknames?" Mary asked. "Venom Kenum?"

The men stared back at her.

Finally, Braggs spoke for the group.

"That guy's bad news," he said. A low whistle followed his comment.

"Don't follow up on that one, unless you want to go out to Chino."

"A regular Boy Scout, huh?" Mary said.

"Well, he sure knew how to use a knife," one of the men said. "He cut up a woman one night. Raped her. Murdered her. Claimed his doctor gave him the wrong medication."

"Anyone know if he's still alive?" Mary said.

"Doubt it."

"That his real name? David Kenum?"

"Far as we know," one of the men said.

"You know, he didn't get life," the tall guy said. Prescott was his name.

"Why not?"

"The whole medication thing."

"What'd he get?"

"Something like 80 years."

"I heard he didn't have to serve it all, though."

"How would you know?"

Prescott looked around the room.

"I heard he got out last week."

M ary started with David Kenum. The guy who had already killed once. And as much as she believed that some people could change, the coincidence in this case was too great to ignore.

She ran his name through her programs and knew it would take several hours to get back all of the results. Mary desperately wanted to use Jake for research, but she wasn't yet ready to tip him off.

In the meantime, while she waited for Kenum's information, Mary turned to the old guys themselves.

One by one, she used her notes to check them off. Prescott. Castro. Reihm. She had no way of determining guilt or innocence, she simply sought confirmation that they were the people they said they were.

Two hours later, she had managed to confirm the basic details of all the men in the room, as well as Harvey Mitchell, who had not been in attendance.

Satisfied that Brent's gang was at least superficially verified, she then turned to the files.

And started with the least likely first.

It took two phone calls and one visit to a public records website to confirm that Martin Gulinski, a.k.a. Martin Gulls, had in fact died, leaving at least one son in Portland. Mary took the Gulinski folder and filed it with the others that she had eliminated as possibilities.

She did as much as she could with Marie Stevens. The manager of Forest Hills told her that there was a Marie Stevens "resting" there, but inquired as to which one she was interested in. When Mary described what she needed to know, he cut her off and said that kind of information wasn't allowed over the phone.

Mary accepted the fact that she would have to drive out there and speak to the guy in person. She tried to find out more about Marie Stevens, including records of arrests in California and public information regarding mental institutions, but to no avail. However, she felt reasonably confident that one of the Marie Stevenses at Forest Hills would be the one she was looking for.

So she set that folder aside, instead of filing it.

Matt Bolt. One unofficial visit to a Union website confirmed that a Matt Bolt was employed in the Los Angeles area. The site listed an address and a phone number for Mr. Bolt.

She called the number.

"Hello?" a woman said.

"Hi, I'm looking for a Matt Bolt."

"Oh, yes. Who is calling?"

"I'm a secretary with the union," Mary said. "I just need to confirm his withholding allowances."

"Okay, hold on."

Mary heard the phone being put down, the sound of a

television's volume being lowered, and then a gruff voice came on the phone.

"'lo?"

"Mr. Bolt?"

"Yeah?"

"Fatty Matty?"

A sigh. "Who is this?"

"My name is Mary Cooper. I'm a relative of Brent Cooper."

"Ah. I heard he's dead."

"Last time I checked, yes, he was."

Bolt gave a little grunt, not of apology, just recognition.

"Had you kept in touch with him at all, Mr. Bolt?" Mary asked.

"Why? What is this?" he asked.

"In addition to being Brent's niece, I'm a private investigator and have been asked by some of his associates to aid the police investigation. Now, tell me..."

"What am I, a suspect?"

Mary didn't even bother answering that one.

"You watch too many movies, lady." Bolt laughed.

"Thanks for your input," she said. "Now, do you know anything at all about my uncle? Anything that could help me in the course of the investigation?"

"Look, honey, I've been in New Zealand for the past two months shooting a film called TO THE LAST BONE. I just got back yesterday. You can check with my boss, or my union or whatever. I wasn't even in town when he was killed."

"So you do porno?"

"What?"

"TO THE LAST BONE. It's a porno flick?" Mary said.

"No! It's not porno. It's an action film. Knife-fighting and crap like that."

"So tell me how you made the change from comedy to being an electrician," she said.

"Guess I wasn't funny enough. Look, what do you want from me?"

"Do you have any idea who might have wanted to kill Brent?"

"Lots of people."

"Do any of these people have names?"

"Look, I don't want to hurt your feelings but he could be an ass."

"What about that group you used to run around with? Whitney Braggs, Noah Baxter, Harvey Mitchell."

"Ah, those guys. Why don't you ask them?"

"What makes you think I haven't?"

He didn't answer and Mary heard the sound of a television being turned on in the background.

"What do you know about David Kenum?" Mary said.

"What?"

"David Kenum."

"Have you talked to him?" he said.

"Just through the mail, I wrote him and asked him to marry me," she said. "I'm one of those prison groupies."

"Yeah, right. You're a Cooper. I can tell."

"Stop with the compliments. So? Kenum?"

"No, I don't know anything about the sicko," Bolt said. "The guy's bad news. Killed a girl. That's all I know."

"Did you hear he was out of prison?"

A sharp intake of breath and then, "He is?"

"Yep. Paid his dues. Thoroughly reformed. Ready to be an upstanding citizen."

"Look," Bolt said. "I gotta go. You need anything else from me?"

"Nope, got everything I need."

"Good. Bye."

"Oh, wait!" Mary said. "Is the red positive or the black? I always get those mixed up."

All she heard was a dial tone.

41

N ext up: Ready Betty. Does six or seven guys at a party. Moves to New York. Does a few plays. Marries and dies of a heart attack.

Mary wondered if that was how her obituary had read. She idly wondered about her own obit. Would it be boiled down to a few pathetic facts like that? Worked as a private investigator. Never married. Owned lots of shoes. Killed a couple people. Died of an embolism while trying to sweat a confession out of a teenager.

Nice, Mary. Keep up that positive thinking.

She forced her negativity aside and focused on the task at hand.

Mary used her paid subscription websites that helped her find a couple dozen Betty Schneiders. She eliminated all of the ones that didn't fit the age range. Then she eliminated the ones that had never lived in southern California.

By the time she was done she had a half dozen Betty Schneiders.

Using the last known addresses and phone numbers, she eliminated another four.

Two left.

Within five minutes, she learned they were both dead.

Mary considered stopping. Why not? They both couldn't have done it. But then she chided herself and it took another half hour to figure out which dead Betty Schneider was the infamous Ready Betty.

She spoke with a daughter who told Mary that her mother had in fact died of a heart attack, and that she had lived in L.A., trying to make it as an actress. The daughter had started to go into Betty's life story but Mary begged off. The daughter did mention that Betty had weighed over three hundred pounds when she died. Heavy Betty.

So Mary crossed her off the list.

She pushed back from her desk and looked at the ceiling and took a deep breath.

It was time to go all out on finding David Kenum.

42

Years ago, Mary had been given the opportunity to obtain a username and password for non-classified state of California government websites.

The opportunity had been presented to her by a happy client who also had these same privileges. Although her possession of access to the network was most likely prohibited, there had never been any questions or issues directed to Mary.

Therefore, it was relatively easy to access David Kenum's prison information, at least everything that was deemed non-classified. It appeared to her that everything about David Kenum was non-classified.

It also listed the name of his parole officer.

Mary picked up the phone and called him. His name was Craig Attebury.

"Hi, my name is Laura Bancroft and I'm with Staffing Resources Management. I am doing a follow-up on behalf of a prospective employer who has been contacted by a..." here she paused and ruffled some papers. "David Kenum."

"Hold on," Mr. Attebury said. Now it was Mary's turn to

listen to papers being shuffled. The beauty of the L.A. criminal system: of course the parole officer wouldn't recognize Kenum's name firsthand. He probably had a hundred or so files stacked on his desk.

"What's the name of your company again?" Attebury asked.

"Staffing Resources Management. SRM. Not to be confused with Sado Rectal Masochism."

"Right, right. And Kenum applied for a job with you?"

"No, sir. He applied for a job with one of our clients. We do all of the tasks associated with verifying a prospective employee's information. Everything but urinalysis. That we outsource."

"I see, I see. Um...what's the name of the company where he applied for a job?"

"Our client information is private, sir."

"Figures."

Mary heard him dig through more papers before he let out a sigh.

"Kenum. Here he is."

Mary gave him a moment to breeze through the paperwork and remember the facts about the person he was ostensibly responsible for protecting society from.

"Okay," he said. "What do you want to know?"

"Let's start with why Mr. Kenum was incarcerated."

The parole officer sighed. "Mr. Kenum was convicted of murder in the second degree."

"I see."

"Spent the last thirty years or so in prison," the parole officer said. "He's paid his dues." That seemed to be the extent of Mr. Attebury's sales effort on behalf of his charge.

"I'll be the judge of that, sir," Mary said. "We certainly

don't take murder lightly here at SRM. Shoplifting and indecent exposure, yes. Murder, no."

Mary tapped some keys on her computer, then asked a few more trivial questions before she went for the treasure.

"Under present address he wrote something indecipherable and then simply wrote Los Angeles," she said. "If my client hires him, the first training he'll receive will no doubt be a penmanship course. But in the meantime, do you have his correct street address? I'll need it to mail the necessary forms as I believe my client will most likely offer him employment."

The tumblers fell into place and the P.O. gave Mary everything she needed.

"Thank you," Mary said. "I believe Mr. Kenum will be receiving some good news shortly."

The P.O. had already hung up.

43

On the way to Kenum's, Mary thought about Harvey Mitchell. The only guy in the group, other than Braggs, who'd made it big. She pictured the pompous ass in her mind from when she'd seen him on television. Smooth gray hair. Teeth a little bit too big for his mouth but perfectly Hollywood white. Slightly heavy, but still with that dignified look men with good features can possess late into life.

Harvey was the late night talk show host who had known Marie Stevens the best, according to the old men. Unfortunately, she hadn't spoken with him yet, and he was her best lead as to what may have happened to the Mysterious Marie. Or Crazy Marie as the gang of old men had called her.

Mary called an agent friend who knew everyone in town. After some small chitchat, Mary got the name of Harvey Mitchell's agent, who in turn gave her Mitchell's assistant's phone number.

While she waited on hold, Mary thought about Mitchell. She'd caught his show a time or two, enough to know that

Mitchell thought he was funnier than he actually was. And that he could be demeaning to guests of lesser stature, and annoyingly ass-kissy to the big stars. She hadn't tuned in much after that.

But according to the Nielsen ratings, apparently the older folks loved him.

Mary took the 405 down to a frighteningly bad neighborhood near South Central, near David Kenum's address, while she waited for Mitchell's assistant to take her call. Mary unconsciously touched the Para .45 in her shoulder holster.

"Claudia Ridner," a bright, chirpy voice said through Mary's cell phone.

"I'd like to make an appointment to chat with Mr. Mitchell. My name is Mary Cooper and I'm investigating the murder of my uncle, Brent Cooper."

"What does this have to do with Mr. Mitchell?" the assistant asked, not sounding so bright and chirpy anymore.

"He should be able to answer some questions regarding certain issues in the case..."

"Mr. Mitchell is very busy."

Mary didn't like being interrupted. "My uncle was busy too, until he had his throat slit. Do you want me to talk to Mitchell or do you want the cops to talk to him? Or maybe a few reporters who would like to know about his links to a brutal murder?"

There was a long silence.

"There is a half hour opening tomorrow at 3 o'clock."

"Thank you, and that wasn't so difficult, now was it?" Mary said.

44

M ary put the phone away and looked across the street at David Kenum's apartment building. Lovely. Gray brick falling apart in every place imaginable, with little balconies featuring black wrought iron. Not useable because the windows had bars on them.

Mary knew why Kenum had picked this place. It must have reminded him of prison.

She got out of the Honda and walked to the front of the building. For some weird reason, she felt eyes on her. She didn't put any store in that goofy premonition shit. Or sixth sense crap. But still, she felt strange. Maybe the pasta last night had been bad.

A boy came out of the building with a bike. He bounced it down the stairs.

"It goes faster if you pedal," Mary said. He looked at her, and Mary wondered if he knew she was kidding.

"What, bitch?" the little boy said.

Mary stopped. Had she heard right? Had she just been called a bitch by a kid? She took a closer look at him. A husky ten-year-old. Or a growth-stunted early teen.

"Nice," Mary said.

"Nice rack," he said.

She considered backhanding him but pictured another trip downtown, this time a charge of child abuse and decided against it.

"They miss you at Finishing School," Mary said, then walked past him and pushed her way into the building, through old steel doors with cracked glass and creaking hinges. Kids today, she thought.

The intercom system wasn't functional. Mary knew this because the entire metal face of the system was smashed inward, as if someone with a size 17 EE foot had made the kick of his life.

It didn't matter. The PO had told her it was apartment 525. She took the stairs to the fifth floor, then fished the .45 out of its holster. She held it at her side as she got to the door.

Apparently the guy with the 17 EE feet got around. Because David Kenum's door looked just like David Kenum's apartment building's intercom system. Smashed in and hanging uselessly in the breeze.

Reminiscent of a Pottery Barn catalogue, Mary thought to herself. The only time Martha Stewart would find herself in a place like this would be if she'd been abducted and held hostage – ransomers demanding her recipe for cream cheese mashed potatoes.

Mary took a step inside the apartment, holding the .45 with both hands, pointed vaguely at the floor in front of her. The first thing she noticed was the smell. There are bad smells, and then there are bad smells. This was horrible. Not dead-body-bad, but definitely fecal-debris-bad.

"Eesh," Mary said to the empty room.

Only the stench answered her back. Mary took in the

place: a single large room with a small kitchen consisting of an ancient stove and tall rectangle of dust where a refrigerator used to be.

She moved through the main room to the back where a tiny bathroom with a filthy toilet sat. "Love what you've done with the powder room, Mr. Kenum," she said. Mary was looking at the rings of growth inside the toilet when she heard the soft scrape of a shoe behind her.

She whirled and had the .45's three-dot sights lined up on the forehead of her unannounced guest.

"He's not here, Sugar."

She lowered the gun.

It was the boy from outside.

"You're as bright as you're polite," she said.

"Nice gun," he said. "I like a woman with a big gun like that. Turns me on."

"So, Miss Manners," Mary said. "Do you live here?"

"What's it to you?"

Mary rolled her eyes. "You said 'he's not here.' Who's not here?"

"Santa Claus," the kid said. "Who do you think? The guy that lived here. David."

Mary nodded. "So if he's not here, then where is he?"

"What's it worth to you?"

Mary rolled her eyes again. She took out a twenty.

"I'm not talkin' about money," he said. "How about you make a man out of me?"

Mary ignored the question and poked his palm with the edge of the twenty but pulled it back when he reached for it.

"I used to steal bottles of wine for him," the kid said. "Last one I gave him was just before he left. Told me he was going to work on a boat. Offered me a boat ride."

Mary gave the kid the twenty.

"This boat have a name? A location?"

"It was called the Diver Down."

"If-" she started to say but he cut her off.

"I know, if I'm lying you'll come back and kill me. Big whoop. I almost wouldn't mind seeing those sweet jugs of yours again."

It wasn't until she was back in her car that Mary finally let herself start laughing.

45

A call to her contact in the state's vehicle licensing division told her the boat was registered and its home base was the marina in Marina del Rey.

Mary took the 405 up to Sepulveda, and followed that into Marina del Rey. She wound her way along the harbor until she came to the marina she was looking for.

She parked and walked until she found a small structure on the eastern side of the marina. It had a sign reading "Marina Office" over its door.

"Hello?"

"What can I do for you?" said a burned out, older surfer looking dude with pink shorts, an orange Polo shirt and topsiders.

"I'm looking for a boat called the Diver Down," Mary said. "Guy's a big fan of Van Halen."

"That's before Sammy Hagar, right?" the guy said.

Mary nodded. "Yes. Well before that epochal moment when 'Van Hagar' came into existence," she said.

"Man, Eddie goes through lead singers like I go through flip flops."

"So where is this ode to 70s rock?" she repeated.

The guy sat, swiveled in his office chair, and looked at a chart of the marina.

"Slip 73," he said and pointed in a vague direction behind him. "That's over there."

"Thanks," Mary said and headed for the slips.

"Whoa, whoa, whoa, Jamie's cryin'," the guy sang.

46

The Diver Down was painted red and white. It was about a thirty-footer Mary guessed. Not really a speedboat, but it had two big new-looking outboards on the back.

"Hello!" Mary called out. There was no activity she could tell of going on in the boat. But soon she heard the creak of the lower cabin's door open and a man popped his head out.

"Yeah?" he said.

"David around? David Kenum?"

"Nope," the old man said. "Who's askin'?"

The man had now come out of the little doorway and stood on the deck of the boat. He looked old and haggard. His shoes and shirt were all a dirty gray. He had grease on his forehead. Dark, leathery skin full of deep creases.

"Do you know where he is?"

"How about you try answering my question before asking yours?" he said. His voice tired and annoyed.

Mary paused for a moment. "I'm his fiancé. His *pregnant* fiancé and when he found out the second part, he left faster than he did his deed. Which was pretty damn quick to begin with."

Would this guy have any sympathy for a pregnant woman? Probably not. But it was worth a try.

"Ah Christ, I'm sorry," the old guy said. "But didn't he just get out of prison? How'd..."

"Conjugal visits."

The old man nodded. "Well, he's not here but I know where he is."

"Let me guess. He's in the drunk tank. Or back in prison."

"Nope. Catalina."

Catalina Island. About an hour and half boat ride from L.A.

"What the hell is he doing out there?" Mary said. "Going for horseback rides instead of earning money to buy diapers and baby wipes for us?" She patted her tummy and emphasized 'us.'

"He came looking for a job. His parole officer sent him here, but I quit doing that after the last guy made off with my motors. Luckily I had insurance. But I told him about a guy I knew was hiring, so he said he'd check it out."

"That's funny, David with a good paying job," Mary said. "Yeah, he just loved to work and work and work. Suppose you tell me what kind of "job" that douche bag thought he was going to get?"

"Something that don't require much of a brain," the old man said.

He looked her up and down and this time, Mary did detect a note of sympathy.

"Look, I'm headed out there right now." He gestured toward a stack of boxes and crates that he'd lashed against a rail. "Have to deliver all that to the restaurant. I can give you a ride out there if you want."

"How long will you be there?"

"Long enough to unload and gas up. Maybe two hours, tops."

Mary hopped onto the deck.

"Hit it, captain."

47

L.A. faded into the background like a corrupt memory filed for deletion.

Mary stood on the deck, leaning against the rail, looking out at the deep blue water. It was beautiful, but she hated it. She hated the cold. She hated the depth. She hated the cool indifference it offered.

She hated that her parents had died here.

Well, not here exactly. But 'out here' in the water, cold and alone except for each other.

Mary wondered if they'd talked. Of if they'd already been dead by the time they hit the water. She shook her head. Why was she always so macabre? She knew better. Knew there weren't any answers. If there were, they would have made themselves known a long time ago. She made a mental note: be happier. Be positive. Walk on the goddamn sunny side of the street.

"Wind is bad," the old man said behind her. "May take us an extra ten minutes or so."

Mary turned. He stood by the wheel, on the right side of the boat. A can of Coke in his hand.

"What's your name?" she asked.

"Mungons. Greg. But everyone calls me Mungo."

"Mungo. It's catchy. So how long you been doing this, Mungo?" Mary said.

"1959," he said. "Sad, isn't it? So much life going on either back there," he gestured toward L.A. proper. "Or there," he nodded toward Catalina. "I always felt like while life was going on I was either on the way to it or on the way from it. Know what I mean?"

"It's like being in the middle of a shit sandwich," Mary said. "I think Thoreau said that."

"Not to mention the gas prices are killing me," he said.

"How's your 401(K) doing?" she said.

"That's funny. You're standing on my 401(k)." He took a drink of his Coke. "So how'd you end up with Kenum? You don't seem his type."

"What's his type?"

"Trashy."

"Well thanks for the compliment."

"My advice?" the guy said.

"Yeah?"

"Get rid of it," he said, nodding toward her belly, like he was telling someone to lose a moustache. Or throw out yesterday's newspaper. "Nothing good will come from you having that baby. More people should do it."

"We could do it right here," Mary said. "Just bring over that bait bucket and some fishing tackle..."

"Look, I didn't mean any offense," the old guy said.

"Plenty taken," Mary said, acting hurt. She'd heard pregnant women could be pretty moody. She moved to the back of the boat, pretending to be nursing her wounded spirit.

Mary watched L.A. recede into the distance. It looked so harmless from the water. Not like the sinful, lecherous community it often was. Although it had its decent moments and its unique attributes, too. Like the Getty. Mary loved to go there. They'd even recently had a Jackson Pollock...

Lights exploded over L.A. and for a brief moment Mary wondered if there was some kind of fireworks show going on. But then blackness crept over her eyes and a horrible, all-consuming pain rocketed down her spine and then she was pretty sure she was screaming. The last thing she felt were hands on her legs and a sudden sense of airiness.

"Splish Splash I was takin' a bath..." she heard a voice say.

And then a feeling of floating. Just before the cold wash of water enveloped her.

What...? Mary wondered, before she simultaneously sank into unconsciousness and the Pacific Ocean.

48

I t was the first lungful of water that woke her up. She gagged underwater, heard the sound of the motor racing away and opened her eyes.

A thick wave of kelp was ten feet ahead of her. Her lungs were on fire and she had a mouth full of sea water but she made it to the kelp before she surfaced.

She spewed a mixture of air and water at the surface, and saw the back of the Diver Down, too far away now, but close enough that she could see a man looking back toward where she'd gone into the water.

Mary treaded water and tried to clear her head. She could see Catalina in the distance, but there was no way she could swim that far. She gagged again and felt her stomach heave. Fear gripped her insides and she nearly panicked, her mind filled with images of her drowning and sharks ripping her apart. In an instant's flash, she saw her balcony with her view of the Pacific and her head cleared.

She had one option. To wait. It was a relatively busy area, with sailboats and speedboats and the occasional ferry.

But she was afraid how long she could last in the cold water. Sharks were known to be out this far.

She swam farther into the kelp. Look on the bright side, she thought. People pay top dollar for this. Probably at least $500 for a kelp bath at LeMerigot spa.

"There's the positive spirit, Mary," she said. "Hey, look on the bright side. Sharks generally don't attack in the middle of the kelp. People drown all the time getting tangled in kelp, but sharks don't attack."

Mary put a hand up against the side of her head. It came away pinkish. She hoped that meant there wasn't much blood there.

"Stupid," she said. Someone had been hiding down below in the cabin. She'd been able to see the old man at the wheel out of the corner of her eye just before the attack. So someone else had slipped out of the sleeping quarters, came up behind her, bonked her, and tossed her overboard.

Mary thought of the Discovery channel, of how seals would roll themselves up in kelp to keep them afloat and then nap.

Cold began to seep into her body. Not enough for hypothermia, but enough to give her a summer cold, and those are the worst, Mary thought.

So she waited. She was enveloped by cold. Her teeth chattered, and she was getting tired from treading water. Once, she felt something slick and rubbery scrape against her leg and she nearly screamed.

Just when she thought she couldn't last any longer and would have to try swimming the rest of the way to the island, she heard the sound of a motor.

It was a high-pitched whine, rather than the deep rumble of a boat. Mary peeled herself out of the kelp and swam toward the open ocean. Far off, she saw two jet skis on their way to Catalina.

She swam as fast as she could for ten minutes, as the jet skis came closer. Finally, when she thought she could get their attention, she surged out of the water and waved her arms up over her head. Survival water ballet.

There were two of them, and it was an awful moment when they seemed totally oblivious to her. Mary gathered herself and launched her body out of the water, waving her arms over her head. It was the second rider who finally spotted her. He zoomed out past the leader, and herded him over toward Mary.

Minutes later, they pulled up next to her. They were covered in tattoos and had more piercings than Aunt Alice's pin cushion. And they were the most beautiful people she had ever seen.

"Dude, what happened?" the lead guy asked, displaying a tongue stud.

"What, you've never seen a mermaid before?" she said. She reached out and got ahold of the jet ski's side.

"Lift me up and I'll show you my tail," she said.

"Cool, man!" the guy said and reached out for her.

It was a little tricky, but between Mary hoisting herself up, and the guy lifting, she was able to swing onto the back of the machine.

"We're going to Catalina, dude," he said to her. "Get wasted and then ride back!"

"I'm going to Catalina too," Mary said. "To beat the crap out of a couple of old men."

"Kick ass, dude!" the guy said.

49

F inding a guy with the austere nickname of 'Mungo'
shouldn't have been a big challenge to Mary. But it
was. Because Mungo certainly wasn't really Mungo.

Still, the old man had a boat and made deliveries. Mary
was sure that part of it wasn't a lie.

After her new 'best dude' dropped her off at the pier, she
went to the public bathroom and checked her cut, which
was pretty small, and pulled out the small business card
case she kept in her front pocket. In addition to business
cards, she had an American Express card for emergencies
tucked in the very back.

She went to the first store she could find and bought a
pair of overpriced pants and a matching overpriced sweatshirt, went back to the public bathroom and changed. Her
head hurt, and her body ached. Her stomach was queasy
from all the saltwater she'd swallowed. She wanted to call
Jake. A part of her still felt like she was bobbing out in the
Pacific, alone and bleeding. As much as the idea of hearing
his voice pleased her, the hassle of explaining how and why
she'd ended up here outweighed the benefit.

She needed to sit down for awhile and get her bearings. She went to a place called the Blue Heron and ordered coffee.

No point going to the cops on the island. For one thing, they wouldn't do much. And for another thing, they might call L.A. and that would cause a huge cock-up and she might wind up in the Catalina slammer for a day or two. Nuh-uh.

She sipped her coffee and thought about what had happened. Why Catalina? Just to get her out on a boat? That seemed sort of silly. They could have said Kenum was a sport fisherman or a worker on a cruise line or a shrimper.

The waitress came back to check on her.

"I'm looking for the old bastard who tossed me off his boat," Mary said to her. "Said his name was Mungo and that he ran supplies in here on a regular basis. Ever heard of him?"

"Nope," the waitress said. "What'd he look like?"

"Old. Tan."

"That's all that's out here!"

"Maybe you've heard of his boat." Mary said. "He's a big Van Halen fan, apparently. It's called the Diver Down."

"Let me ask my manager," the waitress said. "He knows everyone on the island."

Mary was about done with her coffee when the waitress reappeared with an older man dressed in jeans and a blue denim shirt.

"Dick Kay owns the Diver Down," he said to her.

Mary smiled and wrote out a huge tip.

50

Following the restaurant manager's directions, Mary discovered it was a short walk to the dock and an even shorter walk to where the Diver Down sat in its slip.

"Gee, it's not like he and his buddy attempted murder or anything and are trying to keep a low profile," Mary said. She shook her head. Bad guys were so brazen these days. Throw a woman overboard, cruise into the harbor, and take a nap. No big deal.

Mary called out, "Hey Dicky, you dropped something back in the ocean." She wished she had her gun, but figured that they wouldn't try to kill her right here, in such a public place. Besides, she knew she could kick Dicky Kay's ass, and she fully intended to do just that.

She waited but no response came.

Mary cupped her hands around her mouth. "Dicky, if you're taking a crap, flush, wipe, then come out with your hands up. After you wash them, I mean."

A couple people started looking over and Mary knew they might consider calling the cops if she looked too suspicious. So she climbed onto the deck of the Diver Down and went straight to the cabin.

Once her eyes adjusted, she immediately saw Dicky. He was flat on his back on the floor, and his body looked like it had been subjected to the infamous Torture of a Thousand Cuts. His skin was literally slashed everywhere on his body. Great folds of it lay exposed, and folded over, revealing deep red crevasses of flesh.

There was a lot of blood.

But the blood seemed to be too splashed around. It covered the floor. And only the floor. None on the walls or the ceiling. Almost as if there was a pattern. She cocked her head.

And then she saw it.

The blood was smeared into letters.

Enjoy the floor show.

51

M ary spent the night in Catalina, but at least it wasn't in the slammer. It took the rest of the next day for the police to get her statement and let her catch the last ferry off the island.

Mary finally made it back to her apartment. She immediately stripped off her nasty new clothes from the island, threw them into the garbage, took a long, hot shower, and went to sleep. In her dreams, she was still stuck in the kelp bed and she started to sink into the water. There was a white glow in the water beneath her and as she sunk deeper, it seemed as if it was rising. She peered closer. And she saw the faces of her parents.

Mary shot up in bed, her breath coming in gasps. It had been years since she'd had a nightmare about her parents. Mary grabbed the phone and called Jake, but she went straight to voicemail. She didn't leave a message.

Mary slept fitfully until morning, then got out of bed, showered again, dressed and went across the hall. She knocked on Chris McAllister's door, but there was no answer.

She went back into her apartment, made some coffee, and thought about the state of things. There was one facet of the case that had stood out to her from the very beginning. And this morning, she was determined to tackle it head on. She made a quick egg white omelet, chased it with toast and more coffee, then locked the place.

It was time to see Harvey Mitchell.

Mary took Wilshire from Santa Monica up into Beverly Hills and for once, traffic wasn't horrible.

Mitchell's office was just off one of the studio lots in a little cabana type building. Outside there was a fountain with a sculpture of a girl doing a cartwheel. There were also people riding around in golf carts.

Mary had chosen the Lexus over the Honda for the foray into Beverly Hills and now she parked it in a visitor space and went to the front door.

She stepped inside and saw the desk before she saw the woman. The desk was neatly organized with an old-fashioned French phone nestled in its cradle.

The woman behind it was in her early twenties, with a rock hard body and long straight black hair.

"May I help you," the woman said, her voice slightly rough and textured. Either affected, or lots of booze and cigarettes. Mary ruled out the booze, this woman clearly worked out. She was wearing a black t-shirt with black dress slacks. Mary could see the biceps and triceps struggling for dominance."I'm Mary Cooper, here to see Harvey Mitchell."

Mary saw the woman start to speak but she spoke first. "Yes, I have an appointment. Three o'clock."

Mary watched as she looked at the book. The woman's name momentarily eluded her, but then it popped in.

"You're Claudia Ridner, right? Mr. Mitchell's assistant?"

"Yep, but everybody calls me Claw," she said, and held

up one of her hands which had some impressively long fingernails.

"Bet you can snatch fish out of a river with those."

"No, they're not fake," Claudia said, ignoring Mary's comment. "And yes, you can go in." She nodded toward the door behind her.

Mary walked through the small waiting area with a loveseat, two chairs, and a curvy coffee table stacked with entertainment industry pubs.

She pushed open the door, which was already slightly ajar, and stepped into Mitchell's office. It was a large space, lined on all sides with glass that provided views of the surrounding greenery.

Mitchell's desk was solid black and solid wood, stacked high with notes, paper, and books. He looked up at her.

"Ah, the p.i. who threatened to go to the press if I didn't see her," he said, his voice booming with a deep richness that didn't get its just desserts through television speakers.

He was dressed in a shirt and tie, Mary noted the blue sport coat tossed over the back of one of the visitor's chairs.

"Thank you for that completely accurate assessment," Mary said. "That's me in a nutshell."

He stood and extended his hand. Mary took it. "So you're Brent's niece, huh? I can see a slight resemblance. You have all of his good, none of his bad," he said.

"Brent didn't have any bad looks. That's why he was so lucky with the ladies."

"I wasn't talking about looks," Mitchell said. He gestured Mary to the visitor chair that wasn't holding the blue sport coat.

"Can I get you a drink?" he asked, moving to the little bar off to the side. "It's almost five, isn't it?"

"Three-thirty," Mary said.

"Close enough."

He poured himself a scotch.

"Club soda," Mary said.

"Boo," Mitchell said.

Mitchell fixed the drinks and brought Mary's to her. He then sat behind the desk and sipped.

"So how's business?" Mary said.

"Good, good," Mitchell said. "Ratings as high as ever. I've got three development deals on the table."

"I'm happy for you. So tell me how you found out about my uncle."

"The news. Just like everyone else."

Mitchell rocked in his chair and stared at the ceiling. He leaned forward, took a drink, then rocked back and again examined the ceiling.

"So tell me about you and the gang," Mary said. "Brent's old gang. Way back when," Mary said.

Mitchell's head dropped down and he looked her in the eye. "We had fun," he said. "I'll tell you that."

"So much fun that someone would want to murder Brent?" Mary said.

"I don't know anything about that. Brent screwed, and screwed over, a lot of women. That didn't go over well with the women, naturally, or some of the men, frankly. Old boyfriends, new boyfriends, brothers, fathers, uncles, sons, you name it. Brent pissed them all off."

Mary pretended to take a drink as Mitchell looked at her, clearly trying to gauge her reaction.

"I'm a big believer in instinct, Mr. Mitchell," Mary said. "And something's telling me that this isn't about a lover scorned. Somebody is killing off people from the 'old gang' as it were. Brent. Barry Olis. Noah Baxter. Dicky Kay."

"Dicky's dead?" Mitchell asked, his voice incredulous.

"Jesus Christ." His face had gone pale. Mary didn't think he was acting. He was scared. But of what she wasn't sure.

"I heard about Noah Baxter. Somebody shot him," Mitchell said.

"Yeah," Mary said. "Me."

"You?"

"Yep."

"Why?"

"He tried to kill me first. And he was a bad dresser."

"Jesus! What the hell is going on?"

"I have no idea. So who do you think it is?"

"Who?"

"Whoever's killing off you old unfunny bastards."

Mitchell raised an eyebrow.

"Just kidding," Mary said. "But what do you think? Anyone from the old gang come to mind? Anyone who hated all of you and wouldn't mind knocking you off one by one?"

"Everybody hated us," he said. "A lot of us weren't stars. But we were writers, actors, producers, behind-the-scenes guys who made it happen. We ended up being quite a power to reckon with. Not bad for a bunch of guys who just started partying together and success just kind of showed up. Not to mention the fact that between Brent, Braggs, and myself, half the hot ladies in Hollywood were getting laid on a regular basis."

Mary rolled her eyes.

"I'm just stating the facts, ma'am," he said.

"Fine," Mary said. "Let's get down to specifics."

"Oh, looks like I got down to the bottom of my glass," he said and went and refilled his drink.

Mary waited until he had returned to his chair. "David Kenum," she said.

Before he could answer, Claudia "The Claw" Ridner poked her head in. "Mr. Mitchell? You've got a pre-pro meeting in fifteen minutes."

Mitchell nodded and waved her away.

"Let's make this quick."

"David Kenum," Mary repeated.

"Oh God. Psycho. Utterly nuts. Mean, vicious, violent. He killed a girl. Probably more than one. He's in prison."

"Actually, he got out last week."

"Oh Lord have mercy on us all," Mitchell said.

"Know where he might be?"

"Fuck no!"

"Think he might be behind all of this?"

"Hell yes! The guy's a basket case. He's probably killed a dozen people we don't know about!"

"Has he ever contacted you?"

"No. Never. I would remember because I would have shit my pants."

"All right. Marie Stevens."

He turned slightly in his chair. The first time he'd shifted since she started asking questions. Mary noted the move.

"Nice girl," Mitchell said. "A little weird. But nice."

"Know where she is?"

"God, I haven't heard from her in twenty years. She just sort of disappeared. That Kenum," Mitchell said. "One time I was banging this girl in the bathroom." He stopped and looked at Mary. "Sorry, but–"

"Don't worry about it. I've heard plenty of stories regarding sex in bathrooms. I was thinking of making a coffee table book about it."

"Anyway – I was doing this chick in the bathroom and all of a sudden I feel this pain on my throat. I thought it was weird. Was I tangled in something? Then I turn my head and there's Kenum. He said he wanted to cut my throat." Mitchell shook his head.

"What happened then?" Mary said.

"Limp dick happened, that's what. I was a horny sonofabitch, but show me a guy who can diddle someone while a knife is at his throat."

Mary nodded. "That's a cute story," she said. "Bet you always tell that around the holidays."

The secretary poked her head back in.

"Mr. Mitchell..."

He got up and breezed past Mary.

"Sorry, showbiz calls."

Mary followed him out.

52

Mary was not proud to admit it, but she was somewhat ambivalent about kids. She had a feeling she would be crazy about her own if she ever had any, but at the moment, there wasn't a huge attraction there. Some kids were cute as hell. Beautiful, actually. And she did encounter a flare of envy now and then. But she also saw the other side of the coin. The incredible amount of hard work it entailed. She didn't think she could handle it. At least, not right now.

It really came down, though, to her own thoughts about herself as a mother. It was tough to picture. Being honest with herself, she was about as nurturing as Cruella deVille. Maybe the sight of her own little duckling would bring out her soft side, or at least, help her discover it.

Maybe she'd feel more optimistic about her abilities to be a mother if she ever found the right guy. Yeah, right. Like the guy across the hall who she hadn't seen in a couple of days. She must have scared him off.

She stomped on the Lexus's accelerator and shot onto the 405. The hell with Wilshire or Santa Monica Blvd. She was going back to a certain apartment building frequented by a smart-ass kid. And this kid in particular, she really, really didn't like.

Twenty minutes later, she parked two blocks away from Kenum's grungy apartment building. She was behind a beater truck that had a paint-splattered ladder in the bed. Mary parked just a hair farther away from the curb than the truck so she could watch the front of Kenum's building, but remain virtually out of sight.

She sat back and waited. It took almost two hours before the kid showed up.

Mary jumped out of the car, jogged up the street, and ambushed the little smart ass just as he was about to go inside the building.

"Hey, remember me?" she said.

The kid turned and rolled his eyes. "Aw, Christ."

"Close, but the name is actually Mary. Christ's mother."

He started to open the doors to the building, but Mary had climbed up next to him and she put her hand on the door.

"You're not funny," he said. "You're hot. But you're not funny."

"Aw, stop, you're such a sweetie," Mary said. "So who told you to send me down to the boat?"

The kid shook his head. "Don't know what the hell you're talking about. That's a pretty mouth you got, though. Why not put it to better use?"

Mary stepped in, grabbed the kid, and pushed him back against the door.

"Listen you little shit," she said. "Give me a name or I'll take you around back to the alley. And not to fool around, you understand?"

The kid nodded his head as best he could. He even let out a little fart.

Mary let go, slightly. "David Kenum. Where is he?"

The kid gasped for breath.

Mary waited a moment, impatient.

"Where. Is. He," she said.

The kid looked at her, then a sheepish little smile crossed his face.

"Right behind you."

53

D uct tape was really an unfortunate invention, Mary thought. It seemed like a crutch for people who didn't know how to fix something properly. Take tying someone up, for instance. There were all kinds of things a person could use. Rope. Plastic ties. All much easier to use. But David Kenum, he was a duct tape kind of guy.

"Big surprise," Mary said under her breath. Yeah, no duct tape across the mouth yet. But Mary figured that would come next.

"I didn't catch that," Kenum said.

Mary studied Kenum for a moment. He had the body of a forty-year old. Lean but muscular. Only in his face did he look his true age. He had a shaved buzz cut. And sleeves of tattoos.

"I just said how much I like duct tape," Mary said. "Perhaps the world's most versatile product."

"Smart ass, huh?"

"Me? Smart ass? No. But great ass? Hell yeah."

Kenum didn't even smile, just gave a small nod. "Funny. You remind me of Coop. Brent. Your uncle."

"I hate it when people say that."

"He was a dick, wasn't he?"

"I can't speak ill of the dead." She paused. "At least he didn't turn some young girl into sashimi like you did."

She watched him but he showed no reaction.

Whether Kenum was pissed or not, Mary didn't know. But for some reason, he wasn't adding a swatch of duct tape across her mouth.

"And then you did the same thing to ol' Dicky Kay," she added.

"Who?"

"Don't disrespect his memory," Mary said. "That's bad karma."

Kenum looked at her, sharp interest in his eyes. "What do you mean?"

"I mean someone took a filet knife to him and butterflied him. Put some lemon and butter on him and he's ready for the grill."

"Huh," Kenum said.

"Let me guess, you had nothing to do with it?"

Kenum sighed. "I thought prison was violent. This is ridiculous."

"Hey, you mentioned my uncle earlier, why did you kill him?" Mary said.

Kenum pulled a chair up across from her, swung it around, and sat backwards on it, facing her and the door.

"I'd like to ask some questions," he said.

"Shoot," Mary said. "By shoot, I mean ask."

"Let's start by you telling me why you've been looking for me."

Mary smiled. "I just thought since Brent was my uncle, and you killed him, that we have a lot in common. Maybe we could start a book club."

Kenum shook his head.

"I didn't kill your uncle," he said.

Lies, lies, and more lies, Mary thought. But he didn't look like he was lying. And why would he? How could she possibly be a threat to him now?

"No?" Mary said. "Then why did you pay the kid to send me to the boat and have Dicky turn me into bait?"

"I didn't."

"Mm hmm. Just like you didn't kill that girl way back when."

"I didn't."

"Spoken like a true convict. Prison is filled with innocent men, right?"

Kenum shook his head. "No. It's filled mostly with rotten, guilty scum. But there are a few innocents in there. More than most people think."

"And you're one of them, right?"

"I'm guilty of a lot of things. But I didn't kill that girl. And I didn't kill your uncle."

"Then who did?"

Kenum looked at her, but then his eyes lifted over her shoulder. His expression didn't change but she sensed something was wrong.

Mary turned in her chair.

Six figures wearing identical blue suits stood behind her. They all wore Richard Nixon masks.

"I'm guessing they did," Kenum said.

othing happened for a moment. No one spoke.

And then two things happened at once. Kenum lifted his shirt and pulled a small automatic from his waistline. Simultaneously, the Nixon in the middle lifted his arm to reveal an automatic with a silencer attached.

The Nixon's gun spat first.

Kenum's gun fell without firing. Along with its owner, who now sported a red hole just above his right eye.

"Guys," Mary said. "You're doing it all wrong. Presidents *get* assassinated. They don't *do* the assassinating."

Nixon with the Silencer pointed the gun at her while two others approached her. Another one pulled out a sawed off shotgun, jacked a shell into the chamber, crossed the room, and pressed the barrel against Mary's temple.

Mary took the opportunity to study her captors a bit more closely. When they had first come in, she thought they were dressed identically. But now she saw that wasn't the case. Yes, they all had on blue suits, white shirts, and dark ties. But some of the suits were pinstriped. Some had subtle checks. Some of the ties were dark red. Some were light blue. One didn't have a tie. The black shoes differed the most. Mary saw wingtips, loafers, and walking shoes.

But most of all, Mary noticed the hands. They were all old, some wrinkled, most with liver spots, some with arthritis.

One of the Nixons stepped in front of her, pulled out a knife, and cut the duct tape holding her legs to the chair. They stood her up, then tore the chair from her and sent it sailing across the room.

"I wanna do her," the lead Nixon said.

"We don't have time," one of them responded.

"I'm not really in the mood, guys," Mary said.

One of the Nixons grabbed her arms.

"You didn't learn from Watergate, did you?"

A Nixon took out a pair of handcuffs, freed Mary's arms, then quickly cuffed her wrists to a pipe that ran the length of the room.

And then Mary saw something that took her breath away.

One of the Nixons was unbuckling his belt.

"I'm not in the mood, guys," Mary said. "No really does mean no."

Mary shivered. Whatever they had in mind scared the hell out of her.

"I only date younger men," Mary said. "Isn't there a shuffleboard tournament somewhere?" Her heart was thudding in her chest and her mouth was dry. The adrenaline pumped into her blood and she pulled on her restraints.

"Who wants to go first?" one of the Nixons said, his voice muffled and unrecognizable through the mask.

"Why don't you talk about it?" Mary said.

"Someone do her so she shuts up," the lead Nixon said.

"Enough with the sweet talk," Mary said.

She tried to slip her wrists through the handcuffs. She pulled until she felt the cuffs dig through her skin and begin to split her skin and crush her bone. Panic welled up inside her. Suddenly she felt a hand on her ass. Mary kicked back and her foot connected with what felt like a solar plexus. She reefed back on the handcuffs, but her hands caught. A slight metallic grinding sound caught her ear, though. The pipe had moved, sending puffs of rust to the floor.

Mary wrapped her hands around the pipe itself and studied it. She saw a spot weld two feet in front of her, and a bracket with a screw that had already separated from the wall. She leaned forward and lunged sideways, pulling on the pipe with everything she had.

"Whoa, Nellie!" one of the Nixons said.

The pipe had separated completely from the wall, but had remained intact.

"Come on," one of the Nixons said. "Hurry up, I've got a five-thirty tee time."

Mary felt hands on her hips and her mind shrieked with panic and she felt a blind white hot fury explode within her.

She arched her back and rammed backward with her hips, knocking the nearest Nixon back. She pulled the pipe away from the wall and down, then swung around and planted her right foot on top of the pipe. The pipe groaned.

"Watch it!" one of the Nixons shouted.

Mary hopped on top of the pipe with both feet and it snapped, sounding like a gunshot. A three-foot section came free in her hand.

"Shit!" one of the Nixons said.

Mary twisted and swung the pipe in one smooth rotation. She followed through and saw the pipe connect with the nearest man's temple. He flopped backwards onto the floor.

It was like a hand grenade had been dropped into the middle of the room.

Most of the Nixons bolted for the door, but the one who'd shot Kenum went for his automatic.

Mary leapt across the room and brought the pipe down on his forearm, just as he came up with the gun. It fired into the floor and then flew across the room.

She wheeled, looking for the Nixon with the shotgun, only to face the barrel two inches from her face. She ducked as the gun roared. The sound was deafening in the room and she heard the shotgun pellets punch a hole in the plaster wall. Mary swung the pipe and clipped the Nixon with the shotgun at the ankles. He staggered, and she swung at the other ankle, then upward.

The Nixon dropped the shotgun and ran for the door.

Mary thrust the pipe downward and opened her hands. The pipe slid through the cuffs and clattered to the floor. She dove for the shotgun, clamped the stock between her knees and racked a shell into the chamber.

She rolled just as the killer Nixon went for his automatic. Mary fired from a sitting position and the blast tore a fist-sized hole in the plaster just above the man's head. He ducked, gave up the idea of getting back the automatic, and ran for the door.

Mary flipped the shotgun down, caught it by the pump, jacked the shell, flipped it back up, and fired just as the Nixon framed the door.

The pellets shredded his ass and she heard him scream, then tumble down the stairs.

Mary jumped to her feet, racked another shell, and ran toward the landing.

She made it there just as the Nixons ran through the door, helping the one with the bloody ass. She fired again, but hit the doorjamb and saw splinters explode.

Mary pumped the shotgun, but it was empty. She ran back into the room, grabbed the automatic with the silencer, heard an engine roar and tires squeal, then ran down the stairs.

She burst through the doors and onto the sidewalk. The street was empty.

"Now that's what I'm talkin' about, babe," the kid on the bike said.

Mary lowered the gun to her side, realized her shirt was torn and hanging open.

"You're giving me a boner," he said.

"Merry Christmas," she said.

Mary walked back up into the room and found her cell phone. She punched the buttons from memory.

"Cornell," Jake answered.

"I'm half-naked and wearing handcuffs. Get over here," Mary said.

M ary stood in the silent room. It stunk of blood and gunpowder.

She looked over at Kenum sprawled out in an ever-widening pool of blood and felt sick to her stomach. The shock of what had just happened made her numb.

She went over and searched his pockets. Nothing.

Mary did her best to fix her shirt. Her legs were quivering, and she felt a little lightheaded. The adrenaline was wearing off, leaving shaken nerves in its place.

Maybe it was because she was still stunned by the sight of a man being gunned down in front of her, and maybe it was the fact that she'd had five senior citizens assaulting her and rubbing up against her, but it seemed like only a few seconds before she heard her name being called.

"Mary," the voice said.

"Mary."

She looked up, and saw Detective Jacob Cornell.

"Mary, what happened?" he said. "Are you okay?"

She wished he would put his arms around her.

"I guess I'm not an orgy kind of girl," she said.

Jake put his arm on her shoulder. She moved a little bit closer toward him. Mary felt Jake's body heat, and her shivering subsided.

"It's okay to need someone, Mary," he said. "Even if it's me."

Her body relaxed and she opened her mouth to say something like she needed him as much as she needed a trip to the Nixon library. But she didn't. She slipped her arms around him and pulled him closer.

The ambulance team arrived and raced past them.

"Let's get out of here," Jake said. They crossed the room together and were just about to the door when Sergeant Amanda Davies appeared.

"Ah, Cooper," she said. "Always seem to find you in such pleasant circumstances."

Mary felt the woman's eyes notice how close she and Jake were standing.

"I thought I was attending a bat mitzvah," Mary said. "I knew there was going to be blood but this was ridiculous."

"They don't do circumcisions at bat mitzvahs, Mary," Jake said.

"Yeah, okay," Mary said. "Thanks for the Jewish education there, Yentl."

Davies ignored her and said, "Let's take this out into the hallway, unless you want to do this downtown."

"You know, it doesn't really matter where we go," Mary said to Davies. "As long as I'm with you, I'm happy."

Once the paramedics had checked out Mary, and the crime scene techies had arrived, the questioning began.

"So Mary," Jake said. "Why don't you just start at the beginning?"

"Because I don't want to?" Mary said.

Jake just watched her, his face committing nothing.

Mary sighed and explained how she had come to be at Kenum's apartment, leaving out the Catalina side trip, and the little kid with all the information. Just enough to satisfy them, not enough to actually tell them anything.

"So you want me to believe," Davies said. "That there was murder and an assault on you by a bunch of old men wearing Richard Nixon masks?"

"It's just so weird," Jake said. "Nixon masks."

"Yeah," Mary said, nodding toward Davies. "Almost as scary as the one she's wearing now."

"Cute," Davies said.

A coroner's assistant walked past them and down the stairs, carrying a camera and a thick sheaf of notes.

Moments later, the body of David Kenum passed by them on a gurney.

"I'll catch up with you later," Mary said to the corpse. "Now, are we done here?" she said, looking at Jake.

"Could you excuse us, Detective Cornell?" Davies said. Jake looked between the two and then turned to head down the stairs.

Mary turned to Davies. "I'm glad you got rid of him – he's such a third wheel!"

"Shut up, Cooper," Davies said. "Listen, I could care less about you and your pathetic little games with Cornell, but once you start messing with my job then I get angry. And if I find out that you've withheld information or kept me out of the loop on anything regarding this case, you will never work again as a private investigator," Davies continued, her teeth clenched. "You'll just be a desperate old maid."

"That threat's as tired and worn out as your dildo collection," Mary said.

Davies spun on her heel and pounded down the stairs. Her footsteps echoed in the empty hall.

57

It hurt to open her eyes, to sit up in bed, to realize how much she'd had to drink the night before. But most of all, it was agonizing to remember the nightmares: horny old men coming at her from all directions.

The capper, the image that had finally jolted her wide awake at five o'clock in the morning: Richard Nixon. Standing on the steps into the Presidential helicopter. His arms held wide, his fingers forming two giant peace signs.

And he was buck naked.

Mary sat on the edge of her bed. She didn't want to stand up, but she didn't want to lie back down.

And she wasn't going to lie to herself. The Shark's departing shot at her had hit home: '...a lonely old maid...'

It wasn't that she was lonely. Some days? Sure. Once in a while. But it was more the fear that she would become lonely when it was too late to do anything about it. That did trouble her.

The doorbell rang, forcing her to make the decision to stand up.

She walked slowly to the door, her head feeling like an Alaskan buttercup squash.

"Hey," Chris McAllister said when she opened the door after first looking through the peephole.

"Hey," Mary said, her voice flat and tired.

"Um, I was going to walk up to Peet's Coffee – did you want me to grab you a cup or anything?"

Jesus, this guy was unbelievable. And blessed with perfect timing.

"Yes," Mary said. "The biggest, strongest coffee they have, please. Here, let me grab my purse."

Chris smiled. "No, no, it's on me. I'll be back in ten minutes."

"Okay, thanks," Mary said.

She closed the door and made her way to the bathroom. She popped three Tylenol then stood under a blazing hot shower for as long as she could stand it.

By the time she was dressed in jeans and a UCLA sweatshirt, Chris was back with her coffee.

They sat together at the kitchen table, both slightly angled toward Mary's view of the Pacific.

"I like this side of the building better," he said.

"The view could be worse," Mary said.

"I wasn't just talking about the view," he said. And smiled at her.

"Ordinarily, I love morning innuendo," Mary said. "But this coffee is the only thing separating me from rigor mortis."

"Rough night?" he said.

"Rough day. Rough night."

He nodded and sipped his coffee. "I hear you're a private investigator," he said. He smiled, his eyes conveying the excitement he felt of talking to a real-live p.i.

"I'm afraid I am," Mary said. "I got my license through correspondence school. I had a double major: private investigation and seamstressing."

"What's your current case? Or can't you tell me?"

"Umm, it's..."

"I was kidding, you don't have to tell me..."

"No, it's just, it involves family, and someone was hurt, and I'm trying to find the person who did it."

"Oh, wow, I didn't mean to pry. Are you...close to catching him?"

"It sure doesn't feel like it," Mary said, rubbing her head. "Sorry, I don't have a lot of anecdotes..."

"Hey, that's okay, maybe next time we..." he paused, embarrassed about what to say. "...have dinner, you can tell me some stories."

"I don't have good stories. Good neighbors. But not good stories."

He actually blushed a little bit.

"You know what happened between us, the other day..." she said.

"Did something happen?" he said with a small smile.

"Yeah, well–"

"Okay, Mary, I understand," he said.

"You do?"

"Yeah, I know what happened isn't common for you. And it sure as hell isn't common for me."

Mary set her coffee down and looked at him.

He got her sense of humor. He was handsome. He seemed to be nice.

Uh-oh, she thought.

I'm in trouble.

58

L ater that afternoon, she was outlining the progress of the case and still thinking about Chris McAllister when Jake called.

"Let's get some sushi," he said.

"Let's not."

"Oh, come on. You love raw fish and seaweed."

"Stop with the sweet talk."

"Sushi King sound good?"

The Sushi King was a cheap sushi place on Wilshire she and Jake used to go to on a regular basis. Not the best place in L.A. for sushi, but not the worst, either.

"Is salmonella all I'll get out of this deal?" Mary said.

"What, now you need a special reason to see me?"

"Actually, I just need *a* reason to see you."

"Why this sudden shift in Jake policy?"

"Because it strikes me as odd," Mary said. "I haven't gotten a lunch or dinner invitation from you in quite some time. I believe one of the reasons you fell so desperately in love with me was my curiosity. And as you can see, it still functions quite powerfully. So I'm wondering, why the offer now? Are you looking for a little quid pro quo?"

"Your cynicism saddens me, Mary."

"Your sadness makes me cynical, Jake."

"Are you done now?" Jake said.

"No."

"There will be something besides food you'll appreciate. And no, I don't mean me."

59

If she'd been at the Hump, her favorite sushi place in L.A., she would have ordered the sashimi, and had it while watching Tom Cruise take off in his P-51 Mustang from the little Santa Monica airport, just off of where the Hump was located.

But this was the Sushi King.

So she ordered a spider roll and an Asahi Dry.

Jake's order took a full three minutes for him to complete.

"You know, the ocean's fish resources are scheduled to be depleted by 2050. You're not helping," Mary said.

"You're supposed to have fish three times a week – I have it once but eat three times as much," he said.

"Very efficient," Mary said. "So why the luxurious offer to this swanky place?"

"I just wanted to check out your body again close up," he said.

"Very sensitive, Jake," Mary said. "A woman barely survives an assault and you immediately start leering at her. I hope you're not the department's grief counselor."

"Oh, come on," he said. "I'm surprised any of those old bastards survived. I can't believe you only shot one. You must be getting old."

"It's sort of hard to be menacing when you're buck naked. Except for your girlfriend, Davies."

The waitress brought Mary's beer and Jake's sake.

"She's not my girlfriend," Jake said, after the waitress had left.

"So what is it you wanted to tell me?" Mary said. She didn't want to get into this again. Maybe it was Chris McAllister, or maybe it was something that needed to be talked about seriously, and she wasn't ready for it. Not just yet.

"I'm dying of curiosity," Mary said. She stuffed a piece of spider roll into her mouth and studied the poster on the wall describing all the different kinds of sushi.

"We have a confession in the murder of your uncle," Jake said.

He glanced up at Mary, a curious expression on his face.

She looked down from the poster at him.

"Was it some loony homeless guy who wandered in to the station from Ocean Avenue and gave a confession for a free meal and a warm bed?" Mary said.

Jake shook his head again.

"Mark Reihm," he said.

Mary remembered him immediately – he had been one of the crew at Aunt Alice's house whom she'd questioned. He'd been the one with the acne scars and the buzz cut.

"So, what, his guilty conscience drove him to confess?" she said.

"Actually, it drove him to suicide. He confessed in a note."

Mary rolled her eyes. "You've got to be kidding me," she

said. "He's dead and he confessed in a note? And you believe it?"

Jake shrugged. "We're checking it out."

Mary started to tell him not to bother, that whoever was behind these killings wasn't the kind to be plagued by a guilty conscience. But she stopped herself. She sort of liked the idea of Jake and the Shark running around, following up silly leads that would go nowhere. That would give her time to find out the real killer.

"Wow, that's great," Mary said. "Maybe they'll put you on the cover of Police Weekly. Or, even better, Playgirl," she said. "Detective Jacob Cornell. He fights crime! He protects society! He talks on the phone naked!"

"Oh, I bet you could picture me naked," Jake said. He smiled a sly smile at her.

She could picture him naked and on top of her gazing down into her eyes. Actually he looked incredibly hot right now, with that stupid little grin on his face. Like a boy peeking through a peephole at the girly show.

"If I want an image of you naked, I'll order the river eel," she said, pointing with her chin toward the sushi bar.

He rolled his eyes. "Look, I'm not apologizing yet again for what happened. You dumped me. I got shit faced and made a mistake. Get over it. In fact, I think you're already over it, but you're pretending not to be so you don't have to admit to yourself just how much you still love me."

She made a face at him, smeared a big dab of wasabi on her salmon and popped it into her mouth. The wasabi's heat made her eyes water and her face flush. Which is what she'd hoped for, because she knew she was blushing. Jake was right, but she didn't want to admit it. Mary felt embarrassed and a little ashamed of herself, which had probably been Jake's intention.

He watched her with that stupid grin on his face. It was getting wider.

He glanced up at the waitress and got her attention. "More sake, please," he said. "Lots more."

60

M ary snapped her eyes open, saw her bedroom wall, and realized she'd been having a nightmare. A nightmare where a bunch of old men hyped up on Viagra had their way with her over and over again.

"And I thought I'd seen it all," she said, as she swung out of bed.

She showered and drove to Aunt Alice's house. The owner of the house was parked on the couch, watching Animal Planet.

"What do you know about Mark Reihm?" Mary asked.

"Limp-dicked wussy," Alice said, without taking her eyes from the television.

"Nice," Mary said. "Very colorful."

"Thank you."

"So could he kill someone?"

"With his breath, yes."

Mary took a deep breath. Dealing with a Cooper was never an easy proposition.

"Mark Reihm couldn't kill anyone," Alice said. "The man

was a useless pile of flesh with bad breath and the occasional good punch line."

"Your memories are so heartfelt," Mary said.

"He was a wimp," Alice said. "Sorry, but it's true. He didn't have the balls to kill anyone. His nuts were probably like mini brussel sprouts. They should make those, you know, like those mini corn cobs in Asian stir-fry..."

Mary took yet another deep breath. "You're absolutely sure," she said. "Well, I don't plan to pursue it, and hope I'll gain a lot of ground on the cops. If I'm wrong, I'll blame you."

"He didn't do it," Alice said. "I'm positive. I know psychopaths are always the guys who the neighbors thought were nice, but quiet. But I knew this Reihm guy pretty well. Maybe fooled around with him a little bit."

Mary raised her eyebrow.

Alice's face took on a slightly naughty expression. "Well," she said. "His last name *was* Reihm."

"Too much information," Mary said.

"Oh, yeah, who'd you have sex with?"

"What?" Mary said.

"I can tell. You don't seem so manly. I figured you must've gotten laid. About time. Was it Braggs?"

Mary headed for the door.

"It was Milton Berle," Mary said.

"He's dead!" Alice called out.

Just before the door closed, Mary got in the last word.

"Could've fooled me."

61

The next day, Mary was arrested outside her office by a pair of young patrolmen.

"Exactly what are the charges?" she said when they placed her in the back of the squad car headed for downtown.

The young cop in the passenger seat answered her. "You're under arrest for sexual battery."

She pondered that for a moment.

"Sexual battery?" Mary said. "That's what runs my vibrator."

The cops ignored her and before she knew it, she was in a holding cell by herself.

She paced the small room. The metal bed frame attached to the wall. The stainless steel toilet. This was the second time in a matter of days she'd found herself in jail. This wasn't a good thing. Not the kind of career trajectory she'd envisioned.

"I thought you told us you were a chubby chaser," a voice said behind her. "Now you're into old guys, too?"

Mary turned and saw Sergeant Davies leaning casually against the door to her cell. Jake was behind her.

"I prefer the phrase fully ripened," Mary said. "Old is too pejorative."

"Come on, Mary, don't you get tired of this?" Jake asked.

"No, as I recall, you had a penchant for getting tired," Mary said. "Is that still true, Sergeant?"

Jake turned and walked away.

"Ronald Clarey," the Shark said.

"Never heard of him," Mary responded.

"Claims he met you at a senior citizens center and you portrayed yourself as a financial planner," she said, reading from a sheet of paper in her hand. "Says he invited you to his apartment where he says you forced yourself on him. He has submitted his clothes as evidence."

"You sent his Depends to the lab for DNA tests?"

"Yes, as a matter of fact," Davies said.

"This is bullshit," Mary said. "He was probably one of the Nixons – one of the old guys who attacked me. They couldn't kill me so now they're trying to keep me in jail."

"We're looking at the two cases as unrelated, for now," Davies said.

Mary was about to answer when she heard the voice of Visa.

"Well, well, well," it said. Mary looked and saw over Davies' shoulder the tanned countenance of Whitney Braggs and the bright orange curls of attorney Joan Hessburg.

"Ms. Cooper, you're free to come with me." The attorney handed Davies a piece of paper.

"If you continue to harass my client by throwing her in jail every chance you get, you may find yourself locked up before too long," the attorney said. "Consider it a fair warning."

Davies didn't flinch.

"Go to hell, Curly," she said.

62

"Until this case is resolved, you have been granted temporary status as a registered sex offender," Hessburg said to Mary once they'd gotten out of the jail building.

"Why didn't you tell me about your...ah...offbeat proclivities?" Braggs said. "And more importantly how come I wasn't one of your conquests?"

"I didn't think you could handle it," Mary said. This day couldn't possibly get any worse.

Hessburg had a small folder in her hands, and read from the sheet on top of it. "Ms. Cooper, according to this, you are to not go within 100 feet of nursing homes, physical therapy offices, and other centers of the elderly," said Hessburg.

"You forgot bingo parlors," Braggs said.

"I'm not hearing this," Mary said.

"My office will be in contact with you regarding your court date," Hessburg said. "I'll have an assistant gather the necessary information and paperwork so it should go smoothly. I believe this is a ridiculous charge designed to provide pressure to you in some manner. I'm confident it will be dropped quite quickly."

"Did you say I couldn't handle it?" Braggs said, his voice incredulous. "Let me tell you..."

Mary held up her hand.

"Lunch is moving from my stomach up toward my esophagus, Braggs," Mary said. "I suggest you stop."

He complied.

63

The names ran through Mary's head like old news headlines of tragic stories. Ready Betty. Martin Gulinski. David Kenum. All eliminated, some of them quite literally, from the picture.

Only one name remained from the list she'd generated with the help of Brent's old gang.

Marie Stevens. The old guys had said that she was buried at Forest Hills. And that Harvey Mitchell had paid for her burial. But Mitchell had said she was crazy and never mentioned where she was buried or if he had in fact paid for it.

The drive to Forest Hills didn't take long, nor did finding the manager of the cemetery to the stars.

"I called a while back about a Marie Stevens," Mary said to the manager, a highly effeminate older man wearing a conservative suit and sporting smokers' teeth. "I recall you said there were two."

"Yes, I recall that," the man said, not offering anything more.

"Can you tell me where I can find their final resting places?"

Mr. Tidy whipped out a walking map of Forest Hills and a slim black pencil. He clicked on a desktop computer, typed in a few words, then circled two plots on opposite ends of the cemetery.

"This is where they are in repose," he said. His eyebrows lifted on the word 'repose.'

Mary took the map and walked to the farthest one first. It was a classic L.A. day – warm and sunny with a sense of foulness in the air.

She still couldn't believe she'd been labeled a sexual predator – and that her prey was elderly men. She shook her head. What a low point in her life. And now here she was surrounded by dead people. Old men and dead people. That was the kind of company she'd been keeping lately.

It only took a brief glance at the first headstone of Marie Stevens to cross one off the list. Born in 1909, died in 1961. Her husband had followed her three years later. No way. Brent's gang was in its heyday at the time, and long after she was dead, when the real Marie Stevens was partying with them.

A two minute walk to the second Marie Stevens also created a black checkmark on Mary's suspect list.

Born in 1966. Died in 2001.

Too bad, Mary thought. Young.

On the way back to her car, Mary thought about her next steps. She could swing by a V.F.W. Hall and pick out a couple 80-year-old hotties and screw their brains out.

Or she could go back to her office and ransack her Internet resources for this Marie Stevens. Being a sexual predator and all, her first instinct was to go for the old guys.

But her sense of duty to Uncle Brent and Aunt Alice led her to the right, and just, decision. Go back to her office and find out what happened to Marie Stevens.

Then go to the V.F.W. and invite some old men to her place for an orgy.

64

As much as she hated it, she excelled at meeting the organizational demands of her private investigation firm. Scheduling, filing, accounts payable, expenses. They were all nicely filed and collated.

So it took her no time to assemble the stacks of research she'd done this far on Brent's case.

Mary brewed some coffee and turned on her office stereo, putting Prince's CD Musicology on to play. As the stuttering rhythms filled the office, she dove back into the history of Brent Cooper and his supporting cast of cuckoos.

What came to her after nearly an hour of intense reading was that it seemed like Brent and Harvey Mitchell were really the founding fathers of the dysfunctional group. Whitney Braggs played a significant role, as well, but not quite as expansive as the other two.

It was those two who had the big house in Malibu that essentially became party headquarters. They had the first paying gigs – as writers on some long defunct variety show. And it was those two who had progressed the farthest and the fastest in terms of success; with Mitchell obviously eclipsing all of them by a huge margin.

But despite her best efforts, she could find no further mention of Marie Stevens. Nor any pictures. Not any illuminating mentions of a Marie, or an attractive young brunette who had a wicked sense of humor and a penchant for booze and drugs.

By the time she hit the bottom of her material and found the top of her desk, it was nearly four o'clock in the afternoon. Mary did some rapid calculations in her mind and decided that she had just enough time to try one last-ditch effort to find Marie Stevens.

She flew out of the office and into the Accord and fifteen minutes later she was at a run-down neighborhood in Venice.

The Southern California Comedy Museum looked less like a public space and more like a St. Vincent DePaul gone to seed. Mary had just read about its grand opening in the local paper. Well, it had actually been their non-grand opening, because it had been cancelled and postponed to an undetermined date.

She parked the Accord and went to the door. Inside, she could see two men standing next to a kiosk. One wore a tattered sport coat with filthy khakis, the other had on blue jeans, a denim shirt, and a tool belt.

Mary opened the door and stepped inside.

"We're not open," the guy in the mangy sport coat said.

Mary flashed her badge. He saw it, and turned to the guy in the tool belt.

"I'm not upgrading my service – just do it so I can turn on the lights without blowing a fuse, please."

He walked over to Mary.

"What can I do for you, Officer?" the guy asked. Mary didn't correct him.

"I need to do some research on a woman who lived here in L.A. back in the fifties and sixties," she said. "Her name was Marie Stevens and she was tight with a group of guys. Brent Cooper was one of them, and Harvey Mitchell was another."

"Look, man," the guy said to her. "This ain't a frickin' research center. It's a comedy museum. One without much electricity," the guy raised his volume so the guy in the tool belt would hear. "And I still haven't seen your badge."

"Look, Brent Cooper was my uncle," Mary offered. "He was murdered a week ago and I'm trying to help find his killer. Can you help me out here?"

Just then, the worker flipped a switch and the lights went on inside the room.

"That's a sign from God, friend," Mary said. "Ignore it at your own peril."

The guy turned and walked toward a door in the back. "Well come on," he said. "You might want to look through this stuff fast. The way things have been going, there's probably an electrical fire starting somewhere. This place will be toast in a half hour."

65

"You got a name, there, Dapper Don?" Mary said.

The guy let out a small smile. "Dapper. I like that." He looked down at his tattered khakis and grungy sport coat. "Dressed for success," he said. He held out his hand. "Carl Michaletz."

"Mary Cooper." They shook. Mary looked around the room. It was piled with boxes of all shapes, sizes, colors, and branding.

Michaletz pointed to a small group of boxes on the left side. "All of my stuff on the comedy writers and variety show writers from that period are here," he said, leading her over to the section. "It's hard to categorize a lot of people from back then, but I did my best."

He pulled some boxes out and opened the lids to all of them.

"How did you wind up here?" Mary asked. She sat down cross-legged on the concrete floor and pulled up the nearest box. Michaletz pulled a floor lamp over nearer to them and sat down as well.

"I did a lot of coke and booze in the eighties while trying

to become a comedian," he said. "By the time I cleaned up and was sober, I realized I wasn't very funny."

"At least you're honest with yourself," Mary said. "That makes you the exception."

She hauled a load of scrapbooks and handbills out of the box and set them on the ground, then began sorting through them.

"I wasn't bad at business management, though, so I started managing some of the clubs," Michaleltz continued. "One thing led to another and I got hired to run this place, at the behest of a very wealthy comedian who doesn't want his name attached to this thing, in case it ends up being a huge embarrassment."

"Very supportive," Mary said.

There was a small pop and then a sizzling sound from the back room. Michaletz got up.

"Well, everything I have is here. If I have time, I'll come back and help you look," he said. "Marie Stevens, huh? Was that her real name?"

"I think so."

"Okay, I'll think about it."

He left Mary to the boxes and she didn't waste any time.

She thought she smelled smoke.

66

Most of the material consisted of lots and lots of head shots. Even more call sheets with names and phone numbers. It wasn't until she hit the bottom of the second to last box that she found something.

It was a series of pictures of Harvey Mitchell. There were lots of them, mostly with other celebrities and a few of him on stage doing different types of things: stand-up, skits, acting.

It was when she got to the photos of Mitchell and Uncle Brent that she sat up and took notice.

Here was Uncle Brent and Harvey Mitchell standing by a swimming pool with drinks in their hands.

And there was another one with Brent and Mitchell leaning against a Porsche.

And finally, the photo that had Mary on her feet, cell phone in hand.

It showed Harvey Mitchell.

And a lithe, stunning brunette with a white dress and ruby lipstick.

Marie Stevens.

In the photo, they had their arms around each other and were mugging to the camera.

But what caught Mary's eye wasn't the image of Marie.

It was the look on Mitchell's face.

She'd never really seen that look on her own face, but she'd seen it on others.

It was the look of someone deeply in love.

67

Mary took PCH to the little village of Malibu, then wound her way up past the estates of Courtney Cox, David Geffen, and others until she reached the hacienda style home of Harvey Mitchell. The ocean fell behind her, the slight haze of the hills seemed to dissipate the higher she went.

There was the requisite Porsche 911 in Mitchell's circular driveway, along with a giant Lexus SUV. The landscaping was immaculate, the home a sprawling expanse of prized real estate. The rear of the house, Mary knew, would have a breathtaking view of the Pacific.

She rang the bell on the huge pine door and it swung open moments later. A chubby, cherubic face peered out at Mary. The woman was Hispanic and wore a dark skirt with a white blouse.

"Hi, I'm Mary Cooper," Mary said. "I have an appointment with Mr. Mitchell."

"Yes, please come in," the woman said. "My name is Elena."

Mary stepped inside and caught the scent of citrus, probably lemon, along with an overtone of coffee.

"Mr. Mitchell would like to see you in the garden room," Elena said. "Can I get you anything to drink?"

"A Boilermaker would be perfect," Mary said. Elena gave her a blank look. "I'm fine, I don't need anything, thank you," Mary said.

Elena nodded and led Mary through the formal living room, a short hallway laid with Spanish tile, and through a set of double French doors into the garden room.

Mitchell sat on a teak chair with a glass of lemonade. A pitcher of the same stuff sat at the center of the matching teak table, along with another glass.

Elena disappeared without a word, and Mitchell waved Mary to a chair to Mitchell's left.

"Ms. Cooper," Mitchell said, his voice low and even. He stood and shook her hand. "Good to see you again. I'm so glad you called for a follow-up interview."

Mary nodded. "Quite the dump you have here," she said. She sat down and ignored the glass of lemonade in front of her.

"Thank you," Mitchell said. His voice the exact same low, level tone.

"Lousy neighborhood, too," Mary said.

"As much as I enjoyed our first meeting," Mitchell said. "I'm quite surprised you requested an encore. I found our last interview to be quite satisfying and shall we say, complete."

"I felt the same way, Harv," Mary said. "But you know, you're quite the stud. Surely you're used to women coming back asking for more."

Mitchell took a sip of his lemonade.

"This is Hollywood, Ms. Cooper. Nothing is as it appears.

Velvet curtains and smoky celluloid," Mitchell said. He waved his hands in the air and wiggled his fingers.

"Actually, it's all digital now," Mary said. "No celluloid."

Mitchell sat before her, calm and still.

"But you were quite the ladies man," she said. "You have to admit that."

"Ah, your Uncle Brent was the ladies man. I was a bumbling teenager compared to him."

"Even in the eyes of Marie Stevens?"

Mitchell adopted a brief look of confusion, then as if a memory finally came to him, he nodded.

"Yeah, I remember her," he said. "You asked me about her before, right?"

Mary nodded.

"No, she definitely wasn't one of these phantom women enamored with my charms that you talk about," Mitchell said. "She was just kooky. I think Brent warmed the sheets with her, though. Maybe Braggs did, too."

"And you didn't?"

"No. Mental defects aren't a big turn-on for me."

He stretched his legs and then stood. "Mind if we walk and talk?" he said. "My doctor says that I should stand whenever I can, as opposed to sitting. Better for my circulation," he said.

"Modern medicine is overrated. Sit and have some bacon," Mary said, picking up her glass and following Mitchell.

Another set of doors led to the backyard, which had a pool off to the left, a fireplace and pizza oven with a seating area to the right, and an impressive garden with paths, topiaries, and a prodigious flower garden.

They wound their way past a small cluster of orange trees and deeper into the garden.

"Marie Stevens," Mary said.

"Boy, you just won't let her go, will you?" he said. "What do you want from me? I had nothing to do with her."

"I love the sound of truth. It has a very distinctive ring to it," Mary said. "Problem is, I'm not hearing it right now. Because I talked to some of your old gang, and they claim you were pretty intimate with Marie. In fact, they said it was you who had arranged her internment at Forest Hills."

"Forest Hills? I've never arranged internment for anyone. Let alone at Forest Hills. It's nonsense."

"Are you sure?" Mary said. She pulled out the photograph and showed it to Mitchell. "Celebrities lie," Mary said. "But pictures usually don't."

He looked at it, no emotion on his face.

"Once I saw this," Mary said. "It motivated me to do a little bit of checking."

"You know how many women I've had my picture taken with?" Mitchell said. "You're wasting your time."

"I think you're wasting my time," Mary said. "I also think you're full of shit. I think all of these murders have something to do with this woman and you know what it is. I think you're hiding it. What, are you in trouble? What happened to Marie Stevens?"

Mitchell looked flushed now, and his easygoing manner had begun to evaporate. He turned and tossed the rest of his lemonade from his glass onto the lawn and then stepped away from Mary.

Now his eyes blazed and his smiled revealed gritted teeth. "You think you're so smart. Your uncle was a total asshole, just like the rest of them. And just like you."

The ice cubes in the grass twinkled, and Mary saw Mitchell's eyes return to her, angling back from some point over her right shoulder.

"The guy wasn't even funny," Mitchell said. "Just mean."

Mary was already moving when glass shattered behind her. Mary hit the ground and rolled, in time to see a body with a rifle tumble from the second story of Mitchell's house.

She had the .45 in front of her and brought it into line with Mitchell when his head exploded into a red Jackson Pollack before her eyes. His body sagged, then crumpled into a heap. Mary crouched and ran, the .45 in her hand. Bullets tore up chunks of sod as she dove behind a low field-stone wall. The ricochets stopped and Mary crawled around the end of the wall and peeked into the distance. She saw a thick stand of trees and then a straight drop-off, probably to another row of mansions below.

She raced across the lawn, zigzagging to the end of the garden. Mary weaved her way through the trees and shrubs until she reached the rear of the property. There was a fence, and beyond that, a drop off to a narrow road.

There was no one there.

68

Checking to make sure Mitchell was dead was not necessary. It's hard to survive when your head is dismantled into several pieces and what's left simply evaporates in a cloud of red.

Mary took a few deep breaths to calm herself and to think straight.

This pattern of people dying around her was going to have to stop soon. The police tend to notice when every time they're called to a murder scene, the same person is there.

She had to leave.

But she needed information. Her instinct told her that Mitchell had lured her out back, and that he intended for her to be the target, not him. But there were two shooters, not one.

Mary raced toward where the gunman had fallen from the window. He was sprawled face down on Mitchell's outdoor patio. A large pool full of blood covered a portion of the flagstone floor.

Mary grabbed the man's shoulder and turned him over.

She gasped. Her head swam and she staggered backward, nearly falling if it hadn't been for the teak table.

The face, what was left of it, she recognized.

And then she began to curse herself. Her insides felt torn up and she wanted to cry. She wanted to bawl her eyes out and scream.

Of course it hadn't been real.

Of course it had been a set up.

He hadn't been real at all.

The dead man.

Her neighbor.

Chris McAllister.

69

Mary's entire body shook. She felt as if her entire being was about to disintegrate. She had to get control. She had to get a grip.

Mary ran into the house and took a few deep, horribly jagged breaths. How would Mitchell have been in contact with McAllister? Not the home phone – too easily traced. Not the computer, too slow. It must have been via cell phone. McAllister probably would have used a disposable phone. Mitchell, so arrogant, probably had not.

Mary was on the move as soon as she made up her mind. She raced back to Mitchell, avoided looking at what was left of his face, then patted him down. The cell phone was in the inside pocket of his sport coat.

She slipped it into her pocket and ran for the house.

The lemonade glass. Mary ran back to the table and used a napkin to wipe off any prints she may have left on her lemonade glass. She felt like spitting on McAllister's dead body, but decided not to. DNA.

Elena. There was nothing Mary could do about her. She raced back inside and then stopped. Mary knew Mitchell was involved, especially because of the way he had turned on her in the last seconds of his life. He had lured her out to the garden, had planned for the shooter to kill her, but instead, he'd been shot.

Mary hurried back through the living room and out the front door to her car.

She jumped in, ignitioned it, and took off.

She was only a half mile from the house when Mitchell's cell phone rang.

70

She hesitated for a second. Answer it, and the caller knows something is wrong. Let it go to voicemail, well, the caller might think something is up, but wouldn't know for sure.

Mary let the call go to voicemail and she drove straight to her office.

Years back she had subscribed to a number of services that were on the questionable side of legality. It's like the Spy stores that sell hidden cameras even though secretly videotaping people is technically illegal.

Same idea.

But one of her favorites of the services was the phone number database. Rather than calling an operator and trying to con him or her out of an address, which Mary had become quite adept at doing, now she simply had to open up the database, type in a phone number, and it would spit out an address. The database itself was updated frequently, one of its key selling points.

Now, Mary took out Mitchell's cell phone and accessed the phone log. The first number listed was the most recent call. Mary checked the voicemail indicator – it showed no message waiting.

She wrote down the number, then typed it into the database and waited while the system did its things. Moments later, an address popped up on her computer screen. She jotted that down beneath the phone number.

It took nearly two hours to go through Mitchell's entire phone library. Most of the numbers and their matching names and addresses she was able to cross off the list, obviously things like Mitchell's office number, his own home phone, and his voicemail. She recognized one number Mitchell had repeatedly called and its corresponding address: the apartment right across from hers. A spy. That's all McAllister had been. Either an employee of Mitchell's or a private investigator. Mary forced it from her mind or she would start crying immediately, and she had work to do. She studied the list and the other addresses she recognized as Mitchell's colleagues or other businesses.

She had a handful of names and addresses that she was not able to eliminate from the list of possibilities.

Mary accessed a second program, another premium software and Internet package, that let her do people searches. She fed the remaining names and addresses into this program and waited for the response.

When they did come back, Mary was able to eliminate most of them quickly.

It was the entry without any history that caught her eye.

It was listed as a J. Venuta. The address was in Venice. The name rang a very distant bell in Mary's head. She knew she'd heard it from somewhere.

A J. Venuta living in Venice, with virtually no history as a human being.

Mary knew she was close.

71

Jake's name appeared on her cell phone moments after the first ring. She was exiting the 10 freeway and taking 4th Street when she punched in.

"Hi," Mary said. "I can't come to the phone right now so leave a message, or for more options, stop playing with your nuts, hang up, and try again."

"Cute, Mary."

"Thank you," Mary said. "That's actually the system greeting."

There was a pause as Jake said something she couldn't quite make out.

"What do you need, Big Boy?" Mary said. "A career advisor?"

"You know, a crime scene just isn't the same without you, Mary," Jake said.

Mary paused before responding. Her nerves were frayed and she wanted to clue Jake in on everything that had happened, but she was worried that if she did, he'd tell Davies and there'd be an APB out on her instantly.

"And the underwear section of a Walmart flyer just isn't

the same without you, Jake," she said, after a deep breath. She had to stay strong for just a little while longer. A homeless man's shopping cart shot out into the street, and Mary swerved to avoid it. Her tires squealed and she hoped Jake hadn't heard.

"So somebody blew Harvey Mitchell's head off," Jake said with a tired voice.

"I bet his hair is still perfectly in place."

"Actually, not. Most of it is gone along with chunks of his head."

"That's too bad. And you thought his monologues were bad before," she said.

She heard Jake sigh on his end of the line.

"Where does Mitchell live, anyway? On Crenshaw?" Mary said.

She swung onto Ocean Park Drive headed for Venice's Main Street. Her heart was racing right along with the engine of the car. It was a challenge to keep her voice level.

"No, Mary, he actually lives in Malibu. I'm surprised you forgot so soon," he said.

"What the heck are you talking about, Jakie?" Mary said.

"Well," Jake said. "It seems there was somebody here when Mitchell was shot. And the physical description sounds an awful lot like you."

"A total hottie with an ass you could bounce a quarter off of?" Mary said.

"So I take it you're not coming over to chat with us?"

"Hey, I'm working and I don't even know where this Mitchell guy lives. I'm way out here in Long Beach," Mary said. "But let me tell you with utter sincerity that it really chaps my ass I can't help out you and Davies in some way."

"You realize that if we get anything more conclusive, you'll have to come downtown," Jake said.

"Oh, of course," Mary said. "I love to go downtown. Maybe we can get some tacos somewhere?"

"Mary," he said.

"Gotta run, honey!" she said. She thumbed the disconnect button on her cell, and tried to ignore the fact that her hand shook in the process.

72

The house was shabby chic. Whitewashed brick with white windows and light blue shutters. The landscaping in front was nice, if overgrown. There was no car in the driveway and the mailbox was empty.

J. Venuta. Mary realized the name was still bugging her. Where had she heard it? At her office? On the Internet in one of the articles she'd read? At one of the comedy clubs? Mary shook her head. It wouldn't come to her.

So she focused back on the house.

No lights on in any windows. But she knew someone lived here, at least recently. Someone who used a cell phone and called Harvey Mitchell, probably more than once.

Someone named J. Venuta.

Mary reached inside her sportcoat and loosened the .45 in its holster. She was still mildly fearful of knocking on strange doors, after the one at the old guy's apartment had proceeded to be blown to smithereens. Her breath was rapid and shallow, so she forced herself to take a few deep breaths.

The doorbell was to the right of the door, so Mary used the solid brick wall to shield her body as she rang the bell.

She heard the resulting chime in the house and waited. Mary looked around the small neighborhood; no one seemed to be out and about. She saw a woman walking a Great Dane.

Mary turned back and rang the bell again, but still no answer. She reached across the door and rapped hard, three times. No one answered, but the door did open slightly.

Now her heart started beating even faster. Ducking into a strange house with no idea of who or how many people might be inside wasn't one of her favorite things to do.

But that name, J. Venuta. Mary knew it meant something. So she pushed the door open and stepped inside.

73

E ven in the dim light, it was easy to make out the bodies.

One just four feet or so from the door. One sprawled in front of a wingback chair. Another slumped against a sideboard. And a body halfway into the kitchen with only the legs visible.

She bent down to the nearest old guy.

Blood had poured from a bullet hole in the side of his head.

Gun in hand, Mary silently walked into the middle of the room.

The killer had come from the hallway, she thought. Had somehow distracted the guys and then silently appeared and started shooting.

Popped the guy in front of the hallway, near the chair. Then probably took out the one standing near the kitchen, and the man by the sideboard. And then the last shot took out the guy who'd almost made it out the front door, but not quite. Four fast shots. Four old guys, dead.

Mary went into the kitchen, stepped carefully over the body.

Nothing there but a wide pool of dark blood. And there truly was nothing else. No soap by the sink. No salt and pepper shakers, grocery lists, food on the counter. It was as barren as North Dakota.

Mary went upstairs and found the same thing. Rooms with just a few pieces of furniture but no evidence that anyone lived there.

She went back downstairs into the living room and thought it through a little more. Mary studied what was left of the faces of the dead men and quickly realized that she recognized all of them.

Prescott. The tall one.

Mark something.

Frank or maybe Franklin. A chubby little bowling ball of a guy.

And the white-haired guy. His last name was Castro.

The last time she'd seen them, they'd all been snickering in Aunt Alice's living room about Mary. Making bad jokes and lewd suggestions.

Well, they were still putting on a show, just not the kind they would have liked.

Talk about escalation of violence. All four of these guys, and then Mitchell.

Christ, there was no one left.

The phone rang and Mary traced it to the kitchen. It was hung on the wall and had a built-in answering machine.

Mary waited, wanting to get the hell out of the kill zone, but she desperately wanted to hear who was calling.

There was no answering message, just a beep.

And then a voice came on.

It was a voice Mary recognized.

"Mary, please..."

There was a crash and then the call disconnected. But Mary didn't hear it because she was already out the door halfway to her car.

She had to get there fast.

Or Alice would die.

74

She drove like Stevie Wonder on crystal meth.

On the sidewalk when necessary, running red lights, blasting the horn nonstop. She managed to take out a couple of city waste containers, a bike, and a newspaper kiosk.

When she got to Alice's house, Mary was pouring sweat and her car's tires were smoking. But it didn't matter, because she pulled off of the street and drove straight into the yard, at an angle. She hit the front door with the corner of her bumper and it crashed inward. Mary's car shook with the impact, and then she was out of the car, gun in hand, sliding across the hood into the living room.

Later, Mary was never able to quite figure out what Whitney Braggs' plan had been. Because she was already raising her gun when he stepped out from behind Aunt Alice, who was trussed up like a Thanksgiving turkey, held upright by Braggs. Had he planned to negotiate with Mary, using Alice as a human shield?

She never knew.

Because she shot him.

It wasn't that difficult. With Alice tied up, Mary knew she wasn't going to make any sudden moves. So it wasn't so much that she aimed at Braggs, she simply aimed up and over from Alice. If Braggs was there, great. If not, she'd try again.

But Braggs didn't move. He only moved when the .45 slug ripped out his throat. He staggered back, his grip on Alice loosened and she sagged to the ground. The gun in his hand fired, and Mary felt a hammer blow to her left leg. It spun her sideways, but now she poured the bullets at Braggs in a tight pattern, high. She shredded his upper chest and he crashed into the wall, sliding down to the ground. His gun dropped at his feet.

Mary limped over to Aunt Alice and freed her. She sat up, rubbed her wrists, and surveyed the destruction in her living room. "I knew I should've gotten Scotchgard for the carpet."

Mary went to Braggs and knelt beside him, her left leg screaming in pain, her sock and shoe filling with blood.

She put the smoking barrel of the .45 against his temple.

"Tell me where she is," Mary said. "Where is she?"

Braggs tried to answer, but blood gurgled in his mouth and then his throat made a horrible sound. Mary saw the damage her first shot had done.

She reached out and wrapped her hand around his throat and squeezed slightly, to compress what was left of the vocal cords.

"Where is she?" she asked.

He made another garbling sound but this time, she understood.

"*The house.*"

75

She should have known. Really, she couldn't let herself off the hook for this one. Mary could have guessed that Marie Stevens would take up residence at the house where she'd been violated.

Because that's what had happened, Mary was sure of it. It just wasn't the typical form of violation most people experienced. It was the kind that could drive a person insane, and plant the seeds of revenge that would take on a life of their own.

The house was a ramshackle structure just off of PCH, north of Malibu. 'Ramshackle' being the operative word in this region of overpriced real estate. The sprawling, dilapidated ranch style beach house was still worth millions, despite its condition. And despite the Porsche parked in the driveway.

Mary pulled in behind it and went to the door. It opened before she could knock. The sight of the woman shocked Mary. Not because of any unsightly appearance or violent apparition, it was simply because Mary had met her.

"Hello, honey," Marie Stevens said.

"Hello, Janet," Mary said. Mary had reloaded the .45 and tied a makeshift bandage around her leg with a kitchen towel from Alice's. It hurt like hell and Mary didn't know how much blood she'd lost, but her head felt funny.

"How's my favorite talent agent?" Mary said. So stupid. Janet Venuta had been the nasty talent agent in the comedy club. The same comedy club where Mary had been looking for the witness who'd had a crush on a female comic known for her leather pants. The old lady had acted half in the bag, but her wit had been razor sharp.

"Come in, Mary, I promise I won't bite," the old woman said.

Mary recognized the face in the picture with the one now in front of her. In the comedy club, it had been dark and smoky. Now, in the unforgiving light, Marie Stevens actually looked better. Beneath the wrinkles and yellowed skin and eyes that spoke of a road filled with nasty crashes, were the bones of a very beautiful woman. Mary could see why her uncle and his cronies would have liked to have her around.

Mary slipped her hand inside her coat and it came out with the .45 resting in its grip.

"The lack of trust is hurtful, dear," the old woman said. "Very hurtful."

The place was just as uncared for inside as out. There was trash scattered here and there, as well as empty beer cans, cigarette butts, and fast food wrappers.

The only place that seemed cared for was a dining room table with a computer humming quietly away, its bright screen the only source of light other than the sun through the windows.

"Nice little place you got here," Mary said. "Love what you've done with it."

"It's as if Brent Cooper had appeared in the guise of a lovely young woman," Marie Stevens said.

"I assume you bought it with Harvey Mitchell's money?"

Marie Stevens sat down at her computer and swung her chair around to face Mary.

Mary sat down in the chair opposite her and put her .45 on the table between them.

"What kind of woman do you think I am?" the old lady said.

"In order to answer that I would have to know what they did to you way back when, in this house."

"What makes you think they did something to me?" The old woman smiled, the teeth were her own, straight and yellowed from cigarettes.

"Why else would Mitchell pay you blackmail, hire another p.i. to try to keep tabs on me and kill me?" Mary said. "And why else would Whitney Braggs try to kill me and everyone else? Obviously, you had them all by the balls."

The old woman sighed. She turned and looked out toward the windows, out at the gently rolling Pacific.

"They raped me," she said, still turned away from Mary. "Both literally and comedically."

"Comedically?" Mary said.

She nodded. "They supplied the booze, the drugs, the sex, and I supplied the one-liners, the skits, the acts, and they took it all." The old woman's voice was thick and raspy. She waved a wrinkled hand in the air. Mary could smell the woman's perfume.

"They took it all and made great careers out of it," Marie Stevens said. "And then when I wore out, they had me tossed into an institution while they all got rich off my work."

The sound of a car speeding by on PCH reached Mary's ears.

"So that's where you were all these years?" Mary said. "An institution?"

The old woman nodded. "Under a different name," she said. "I got out awhile back and began exacting my revenge. I had quite long time to plan it. Give or take a lifetime."

"Some people take up gardening," Mary said.

"Some people needed to die," the old woman countered.

Mary sighed. "So who actually killed Brent?"

"Braggs," the old woman said. "He did the dirty work. I was the brains. But Braggs is psychotic. I kept you alive because I knew in the end, I would need you to take him out. I didn't think I could do it."

Mary nodded. She was angry. Angry about the whole thing. That this woman had murdered her uncle. That her uncle had played a part in destroying this woman's life for some money that didn't last, and jokes that had long since been forgotten.

"But you shouldn't have hard feelings toward Braggs," Marie Stevens said. "I had him shoot that McAllister jerk to keep you alive. Just before Braggs shot Harvey, the asshole."

"That was very nice of Braggs," Mary said. "I think I'll send him a pick-me-up bouquet from FTD."

The old woman looked at Mary. "Whatever Braggs was doing at Alice's house, that was his own plan. I guess to tie up loose ends on his part."

Mary felt blood trickle down her leg. There were now two Marie Stevenses in front of her.

"I'm done," the old lady said.

"Done?"

"I've done what I needed to do. I want to go back now. Call your boyfriend. Jake. That's his name?"

"Go back where?"

"To the hospital," Marie Stevens said. "I don't like it out here. Besides, with this," she said, and pointed at her laptop. "I can send my stuff out. Leno used one of my jokes a couple weeks ago. Under a false name, of course."

Mary put away the .45. She felt funny, almost sleepy. Her foot was soaked in blood and now it felt cold.

"I want to hear it," she said.

"Hear what?" Marie Stevens said.

"The joke."

76

Jake and the Shark arrived minutes later with a whole contingent of LAPD's finest. They entered the room with guns drawn.

"Hate to interrupt you two," the Shark said. "But one of you is under arrest for murder."

"I didn't know reptiles could become homicide detectives," Marie Stevens said, and looked Davies up and down. "Or is this some kind of diversity mandate?"

Mary, still feeling lightheaded and like she was going to pass out at any moment said, "Yeah, she has to sit out in the sun to raise her body temperature."

Davies took out a pair of handcuffs.

"Don't worry," Mary said to Marie Stevens. "Those are for Jake. They have his and hers."

"He went from you to her?" Marie said. "And I thought my judgment was questionable."

"That's enough," Jake said. "Come on in guys." A team of paramedics came through the door and Jake directed them to Mary. He followed them over and held Mary's hand as the paramedics began to set up the stretcher and examine her leg.

The Shark put Marie in handcuffs.

"Bet you'd love a conjugal visit," the old lady said to Davies. "Well, forget it, even if I get 20 years, I wouldn't be *that* desperate."

Davies shoved her toward the door where two uniforms escorted the lady to a patrol car. Davies turned to Jake, saw him holding Mary's hand, and turned and followed the old lady out into the sunshine.

Jake smiled at Mary as the paramedics lifted her onto the stretcher. He still held her hand and stroked her hair.

"That old lady's kinda funny," he said. "For a murderer."

In response, Mary passed out.

77

"This is downright painful," Mary said, taking a long pull of her beer.

"Brutal," Alice said.

They were seated at a table inside the Funny Factory, a small and sparsely attended comedy club in Santa Monica. Uncle Kurt Cooper was on stage.

"I think he's funny," Jake said.

Mary and Alice both looked at Jake.

"That's the funniest thing I've heard tonight," Alice said.

Jake quickly changed the subject. "So they shipped Marie Stevens back to the mental institution today. Unfit for trial."

Mary idly wondered if letting Marie Stevens live had been the right thing to do. She could have taken her out at the house in Malibu. Instead, she had called Jake while she was en route, shot and bleeding.

"Those guys didn't just take her material," Mary said. "They took her soul and her sanity."

"Lots of people got ripped off back then," Alice pointed out. "If people got shot out here for stealing material, Hollywood would have a population of maybe ten or twenty people."

Mary nodded and looked at the stage. "Speaking of material," she said.

They all looked at Kurt Cooper on stage.

"I think his stuff is safe," Alice said.

Out of the corner of her eye, Mary watched Jake take a drink from his beer. God, he looked so handsome. And he'd been so good helping her recover from the gunshot to her leg. Luckily, there'd been no nerve damage. But Jake had jumped right in to help, buying her groceries, cooking for her, visiting Alice, too.

Now, Jake turned and saw her looking at him.

"What?" he said.

She reached across and held his hand. Squeezed it gently.

"Jake. I..."

He waited. "You what?"

"I..." she said.

He leaned toward her, as if she were going to whisper.

She started to say something, then stopped.

Instead, Mary pulled Jake to her and kissed him.

THE END

Read the next books in the award-winning
Mary Cooper Mystery series:

Murder with Sarcastic Intent (Mary Cooper Mystery #2)
Gross Sarcastic Homicide (Mary Cooper Mystery #3)

TO FIND A MOUNTAIN (A WWII Thriller)

STANDALONE THRILLERS:

THE RECRUITER

KILLING THE RAT

HEAD SHOT

THE BUTCHER

BOX SETS:

AMES TO KILL

GROSSE POINTE PULP

GROSSE POINTE PULP 2

TOTAL SARCASM

WALLACE MACK THRILLER COLLECTION

SHORT STORIES:

THE GARBAGE COLLECTOR

BULLET RIVER

SCHOOL GIRL

HANGING CURVE

SCALE OF JUSTICE

AFTERWORD

For special offers, free ebooks, exclusive content and to hear about new releases, sign up for

The Official Dan Ames Book Club:

AuthorDanAmes.com

ABOUT THE AUTHOR

Dan Ames is a USA TODAY bestselling crime novelist and winner of the Independent Book Award for Crime Fiction.

www.authordanames.com
dan@authordanames.com